small as a mustard seed

Shelli Johnson

ALPHA
DOLL

Scripture taken from the HOLY BIBLE, NEW INTERNATIONAL VERSION. Copyright 1973, 1978, 1984 by International Bible Society. Used by permission of Zondervan. All rights reserved.

Song *This Little Light of Mine*, words and music by Harry Dixon Loes, Public Domain.

Book and Cover design by Alpha Doll Media, LLC
Cover image Copyright Utkamandarinka, used under license from istock.com.

Author's website: shellijohnson.com
Publisher's website: alphadollmedia.com

ISBN 978-1-948103-92-3

First Edition, Second Printing: December 2017

For Rollin

November 1965

"I AIN'T AFRAID this time. I ain't some kid don't know shit from Shinola," my father hollered as he stood in the driveway.

In the curve of his chest, pressed tight against the denim of his overalls, he clutched a black revolver. The other hand combed through the short dark hairs of his flattop. My father was six foot two, two hundred twenty pounds, and in the soft morning light, he cast a long shadow across the courtyard.

I squatted in the pasture, some hundred or so feet away, nudging the top of my head around one corner of the barn. I was ten that year, a slip of a girl, short for my age, brown-eyed and dark-haired. Storm clouds blackened the sky and a cool rain started to fall as I watched him crack open the gun's chamber to check that it was loaded, smile ever so slightly, then snap it back closed.

Just a few minutes earlier, we'd all been in the kitchen except for my mother, who was humming softly through her closed bedroom door. My sister Jolene — thin, blonde, and eight years old — had been using a knife to scoop strawberry jelly from the jar. The dollop was too round, the knife too flat, and her movement too fast, so the jelly vaulted through the air and splattered against the floor. What should have been a simple mess to clean up was not. My father stared at the stain, his eyes glassing over. He pushed himself away from the table with a grunt and, favoring a right hip wounded during the war in Korea, stilted side-to-side toward the cupboard. He groped along the top shelf, behind a stack of dusty teacups, and pulled out the gun. He cut his eyes toward my sister and me, gun barrel pointing at the floor, his finger against the trigger.

Jolie's face paled. The knife in her hand clattered to the table.

"Daddy?" I said.

"Goddamned Communists," he answered.

I grabbed Jolie's wrist, yanking her from the kitchen to the foyer, past shoes lined up in two neat rows and coats piled on hooks in the wall. Clothed only in pajamas and socks, we raced out the front door, sprinting toward the pasture where we hid at the edge of the barn. Breathing hard, Jolene huddled up behind me, her body shivering against mine. We watched our father limp toward us, the gun dipping toward his belly before he stuffed it into the pocket of his overalls.

"Goddamn, I ain't kidding." Softer, he added, "Edgecomb ain't gonna bite it 'cause of me."

Jolene slid her fingers against my waist and squeezed. "You got to hide. I'll go to the woods. I'll draw him out. It's me he wants."

"You're crazy," I shot back.

Something in the hay field, opposite where we were, caught my father's attention, and as he stared in that direction, Jolene made an odd clucking sound and whispered, "It's always me he wants. You just hide in the barn and don't get caught."

"I'm not gonna—" But I never finished. She hauled me backward in the muck, shoving me through the barn's side door. The doorjamb framed her for a moment, and then she darted into the rain, slamming the door behind her and leaving me in darkness.

Before I could even get my bearings, the overhead lamps burned oblong patches across the dirt floor. Three or four of the horses nickered softly. I cowered next to the side door, cool air bleeding beneath its bottom edge. I had about eight feet of passageway before it widened into the vast, open expanse of the barn's center. I couldn't see my father, but I knew he must be near the light switch, some fifty feet from me.

"It ain't feeding time," he said to the horses. "You seen them two gooks? Both'd be good, but either one'll do." A minute later, his boots clopped across the sawdust. I heard him snap on the light in the feed room and yell, "Hah!"

With my heart like a jackhammer in my chest, I threw my shoulder against the side door only to find Jolene had latched it from the outside. In the feed room, my father tossed bags of corn and bales of hay out of his way. He said, "It ain't right, them gooks shooting Edgecomb like that."

I gulped a deep breath and crawled to the nearest stall. Our old buckskin mare, her tan coat flaked with dried mud, stared at me. I spotted the darkest corner, ripped a square of hay from the feed bin, and hunkered down so low that my behind smacked into sawdust and manure. I covered myself with the hay as best I could. In the feed room, my father sideswiped a plastic bucket full of grooming tools, their metal edges scraping across the concrete floor.

A point in the center of my head throbbed. My knees ached. I squeezed my eyes shut and pressed my spine harder against the plank-board wall. Head bowed, fingers steepled between where my breasts would someday be, I prayed two things with soft words that swirled feathery puffs of air against my knuckles: first, that he wouldn't see me tucked in the corner of this tiny stall, and second, that if he did, he would get whatever he was going to do over with quick.

Back in the main part of the barn, my father jerked the light switch a half-dozen times. He yelled, "You in here, you Communist?"

My slow, deliberate breathing was enormously loud. I clamped my lips together, but that just made my lungs burn and my face prickle. I remember how everything seemed so thunderous while I flattened myself into the corner, trying hard to be small and quiet. I listened to my father's boots thump across the floor and then stop at the first stall in the line. He worked the latch back and forth, the door rumbling open on its track. Wind blew through the cracks, carrying my father's scent, something strong and thick like burning paper, like wet leaves smoldering in the fall. It was an odor I would come to know later as the stench of his sickness. Above me in the hayloft, a lone cricket chirped, and I thought I'd go out of my head with that sound, a noise so normal in a place where I'd bitten through my bottom lip and blood seeped along my chin, in a place where my bladder had let go and I crouched in a puddle of my own urine.

"You in there?" my father growled. "Come on out and make it easy on yourself."

Hay rustled, hooves stomped, water rushed from an upturned bucket, and then, "Goddammit." The hinges squawked, and my father slammed the latch closed. There was no way out of this stall, no way to make myself smaller, and he was closing and latching, moving on down the line to where I hid, only three stalls away.

My hands bled. Brittle hay, splintered boards, and rusted nails not quite hammered in had sliced into them. I hung so intensely on every sound my father made that I hadn't felt the sting as the skin opened. Only the drip of blood, liquid sliding across my skin, forced me to tilt my head down, and as I did so, some of the hay tumbled to the floor. Rain pounded against the roof, wind rocked the eaves, and my father swung back the door to the stall where I hid.

He stared at the horse, which stood stiff-legged in the middle of the stall, her body at an angle. Between the horse's legs, I could see him clearly — eyes so exhausted that the skin underneath hung in black pouches, rain droplets beaded in the stubble on his face, faint yellow patches on his long-sleeved shirt where sweat from his armpits had stained the white cotton weave — but he seemed oblivious to me in the back corner to his left. It was a side effect of medication, I understood years later, that kept him from seeing me right away. It was simply dim light bulbs and the damaging of his optic nerve; it was not God, as I thought back then, answering my prayer.

My throat scratched. Sweat bumped down my back and pooled in the elastic of my underwear. I took itty-bitty sips of air. The stink of him made my lips pucker, made my throat want to wretch and gag. My father's eyes traced the line of the mare's front leg to the floor. He stepped forward, sawdust puffing under his boot. His cheeks caved inward, his knees bent, and his fingers brushed against the horse's hoof. "Well, shit in a poke!" he said.

He plucked something round between his thumb and index finger, stood up, and boosted it toward the light. He squinted then brought it close to his nose and sniffed. All of a sudden, his shoulders eased and his face relaxed. The look of concentration, that something hard and chiseled, vanished. He grinned into the blank air.

"Well, I'll be damned," he said to the horse. "You shitting nickels there, Roxie?"

He knelt down again, rainwater dripping from his hair, and combed his fingers through the sawdust. His smile broadened. "You shitting a few nickels. Here's a penny and a quarter."

A shiver ripped through me. I knew that next to my hip, beside the hole in the pocket of my pajamas, there would be a small pool of lunch money. Outside, the back door of the house swung open, and my mother shouted about breakfast. She hollered twice before I heard the screen door slam against its frame.

"Where you at?" my father said in a rough voice that sliced through me like a blade.

Air gushed from my mouth as I understood there was no longer a point to hiding. I eked out the word, "Here."

Coins sailed out of his hands, falling to the ground with soft whispery plops. He rushed at me with arms outstretched, fingers stiff like claws. Red spattered his cheeks. The spooked mare snorted and reared back. He gripped my upper arm so tightly that in a little while, I would have purplish bruises in the size and shape of his fingers. He hauled me past the horse, and I got a sight of his revolver half-buried in the sawdust. He shoved me into the light. Standing in the doorway of the stall, I watched his face slacken. "Why, you're just some little girl."

I nodded, my head making a big, wobbly gesture.

He knelt and brought his face within inches of mine, close enough for me to count the pockmarks where acne had scarred him as a teenager. "Well, where's the rest of them?"

"I don't know," I screeched in a high voice, my mouth gone dry. Right then, I thought he'd been asking about Jolene.

He breathed the smell of eggs and bacon over me. "You hiding their weapons?"

Four years earlier, when President Kennedy committed America to Vietnam, my father began muttering about gooks and Communism and war. He would read the newspaper at breakfast then crumple the pages and stuff them in the trash, mumbling all the while about the government sending boys to meaningless deaths. "They're just kids! Kids!" he'd say. He watched television, punctuating the reports every so often with, "Goddamned gooks!" Sometimes when the phone rang, he would startle, ducking low to the ground and clutching his hands to his head.

I didn't understand his words and his oddities had never harmed me, so it didn't occur to me until right then in that stall, his eyes so intent on an answer, his fingers ready to hurt me more, that he believed I was the enemy. My head shook side-to-side, wet hair slapping against my cheeks. "Huh-huh. No, Daddy."

"We'll just see." He scanned the stall and, within seconds, saw the butt of the gun. He faced me again, his grip tightening. He shook me back and forth, saying, "All you gooks are liars, too." He leaned over and snatched the revolver. He slid it under my nose. "What's this then?"

My legs wobbled. I stumbled over words while I searched his hard face for something soft and familiar.

"Speak up!" he yelled.

"Yours," I barked. "It's yours."

"What?"

"It's your gun, Daddy."

He waggled the barrel back and forth, saying, "Soldiers don't carry guns like this."

My hands started to tremble. "You got it from the cupboard in the house."

"What house? There's no houses, just goddamn shacks."

My body felt cold, clammy. "Daddy, please, it's your gun. You brought it in here."

He narrowed his eyes. "How come you keep calling me, 'Daddy'? I ain't nobody's daddy."

Low in my belly, something tightened into a hard little ball. My arms hung limp at my sides. My vision seemed hazy, dark around the edges. My father let go of me and wrapped his fingers around the butt of the gun, easing one alongside the trigger. He raised it from his chest to his head.

Back in August, the television flickered images of a bunch of Marines hoisting their Zippo lighters to thatched roofs in the village of *Cam Ne*. The next day my father gutshot a gopher. He watched with satisfaction on his face as it writhed, spewing blood and mucus, before it died on the warm, soft ground near my feet.

"That's what dead is," he said flatly. "Now you seen what dead is."

Then with the toe of his boot, he'd kicked its limp body into the garden.

In the barn, he thumbed back the hammer. Quietly, he said, "Sing me a song, angel, or I'll pull the trigger."

Thinking he was talking to someone else, I glanced around, catching sight of the sloping backs of horses, the matted fur of my tabby cat, and a dark round circle in the dirt where the rain had seeped through the roof. When my eyes finally fell on him again, he pressed the barrel more tightly against his temple and said, "Now. A song. Any song."

My gut convulsed, my stomach lurched, and a wicked taste filled my mouth. I staggered backward, tripping over my own feet and landing on my behind. My father's eyelids slid to half-staff. He bowed his head like a parishioner awaiting absolution, and one quick, clear thought flashed through my mind: *If I don't pick the right one, it'll be me who kills him.*

I warbled a melody, the same one my mother sang to lull me to sleep. In some places, the pitch went high and tinny; in others, the words broke. "*This little light of mine, I'm gonna let it shine. Oh, this little light of mine, I'm gonna let it shine. Let it shine. Let it shine. Let it shine."*

After I finished, my voice drying up and only the sound of rain and hooves between us, he said, "I ain't got any light left in me. Everything in there's dark and sour." He lowered the gun to his lap, eased the hammer down, and let the revolver slide back into the sawdust. The lines of his face had gone slack. "My girl, Adele, used to sing me that song. Back when she sung it, though, I tried to believe her."

My chest felt like all the air had been squeezed from it, my breaths coming in short, choppy gulps. My insides felt constricted and hot, like an explosion just about to happen. My father stared at his palms then flipped his hands over and glared at the veins, branching like blue, tangled ropes. He fingered a mole on his left wrist, bulging with black hairs. He looked around the stall, lips pursed as he lighted upon sawdust in the shape of my rump, manure mashed down, blood droplets and hay scattered across the floor. He followed a glittering trail of lunch money from the corner where I had been to the ground beside his hip. He stared at the gun and in a faraway voice said, "Huh." He might've added, "How'd that get there?" for all the confusion that arranged itself on his face. He laid eyes on me and said, "Ann Marie? What happened?"

I didn't answer. I pulled my knees to my chest and curled my toes into the dirt. My father rocked forward, and out of pure reflex, my arms flailed, grasping at the ground behind me, and my legs kicked, feet shoving me across the floor. I scampered away from him, and the look on his face changed from confusion to fear. He thrust his palm into the air between us, fingers splayed like a stop sign, and soothed, "Shhh. Shhh. Go in the house now. Please, just go."

MY MOTHER, A woman just a hair over five-foot tall, thick around the middle, her dark hair loosely pinned in a bun, stood by the gas stove and twisted a spatula in half-a-dozen eggs, breaking yolks. The kitchen, a rectangular blue-wallpapered room with an entrance to the foyer on one end and the living room on the other, was quiet except for the sound of popping grease. She banged the skillet against the burner, splashing grease in dark spots against the wall's tiny white flowers. She heard the front door hinges creak and, without turning, said, "Where've you been? Breakfast's on."

In the foyer, water and mud dripped from me onto the thin brown carpeting. I watched her elbow rise and fall as she folded eggs into an omelet. Without warning, my throat broke open with a whining sound like dogs make when you beat them. My mother spun around, and grease flew off the spatula as it fell from her grasp and clattered against the yellowish linoleum floor. She rushed toward me, eyes wide and frightened, arms outstretched. She crouched down, her eyes darting across my face, arms, chest, legs, searching for wounds.

"Ann Marie, what happened?"

Small whimpers became vast sobs that shook my body as she pulled me against her robe, smearing mud, manure, and blood onto the white terrycloth. Wrapping her arms around me, she swayed back and forth, humming something slow and soft. We rocked and I breathed, pulling the sweet smells of her — Ivory soap, strawberry-scented lotion, Aquanet hairspray — into my lungs. After I'd calmed down, her fingers drifted in slow circles between my shoulder blades, and she said, "Honey, where's Jolene?"

I stiffened and jabbed a finger toward the window, where rain was splotching the glass. "She's out there."

"Is she all right?"

"I don't know."

"Sugar, you stay right here. I have to find your sister."

She rose to her feet, and I lunged at her, yelling, "No! Don't go! He'll come back!"

Startled, she said, "Who? Who will come back?"

I scrambled to bury my face against her chest, but she gripped my shoulders and held me away from her.

"Who?" she said again.

I clamped my eyes closed.

"I won't be mad," she whispered. "I promise. Just tell me."

"Daddy," I said, my mouth barely opening, his name thick on my tongue.

"Your *father* did this?"

"Uh-huh," I said.

"Why would he do that?" Suddenly, the pressure of her grip eased and her warmth slipped away. When I cracked open my eyes, she was leaning against the front door, looking out the window. She could've been made from salt for the amount of color she lacked. She said in a quiet voice, "Did you do something to make him mad?"

"No," I said, and the belief I held close, the one where she would roar up and defend me, sunk low, making a hard, tight knot in my belly.

My mother stayed quiet for a while. Rain pelted the glass. Her breath fogged the pane. A minute passed, then two, and she started to whisper like a chant, "Not again, not again, please not again."

I didn't understand why my mother would say that. I wanted to ask her, but smoke rolled through the air, and she rushed into the kitchen to wrench the skillet from the stove. She spun the cold tap and chucked the pan, blackened eggs and all, into the sink. I lagged by the kitchen table, and she turned to face me, eyes red, hands trembling. "I have to find them, Ann Marie. Go to the bathtub and get cleaned up."

I cranked the hot water to full and the cold to just barely open, so as I soaked, my skin blotched deep shades of red. Dirt, urine, and manure sifted into the water, making it murky. My body shuddered, and I wanted to scream, "What about me? What about what *he* did to *me*?" Silently, I ran the bar of soap across the flat of my stomach. I sunk lower, slipping my head under the water until only my nostrils poked above. The water felt gritty against my skin, the porcelain hard against my back. After a while, the sting in my palms became a numb throb.

My mother always said I had fragile hands. She would grasp them in her own, turn them palms up, and say, "Marie, honey, you've got hands that weren't meant for farming. They're delicate." She used to tell fortunes, mostly family and friends, reading the lines of their palms with her brow furrowed as she searched through a tattered book for meanings. She would sit on my bed late at night, her dark hair swooping in curls around her face, and hold my palm beneath the lamp on the nightstand. She traced the lines with her index finger, met my eyes, and exhaled with the word "fragile" slipping slow and quiet from her lips. Then she chose one line, ran her ragged fingernail across it, and said, "This here? This means you'll have a long life."

"But will it be good?" I asked.

She frowned, and her lovely, round face pinched up. "Well, of course it'll be good."

"My palm tell you that?"

"No, your mama tells you that."

"What's my palm say?"

"That it's time for bed." And she shut off the light, kissed my forehead, and never did answer.

The water cooled, and I raised my wounded palms near my face. Maybe she didn't tell me because the lines revealed bad things about my life — my father with a gun to his head, my sister cowering in the woods with her face partly hidden by her hair, my mother choosing her husband over her children. To calm myself, I started to count the heartbeats that pounded against my fingertips. By the time the hinges on the front door squawked and my mother's voice darted through the air, I'd reached four hundred and eleven.

THAT EVENING, NOT long after supper, Jolie and I huddled around the heating vent on the floor of her bedroom. By cocking our heads at an angle, we could see through the grate into the living room. My mother sat half-turned on one end of the couch and stared at my father. He slouched at the other end, watching the television with its sound turned down, gray light flickering across his face. I glanced up, scanning Jolie's face, pausing at a swelled bottom lip and the small, purplish bruise darkening the corner of her mouth. This morning, she'd been brought inside by our mother then had raced up to her room and hadn't uttered a word since. She glared through the vent, her jaw clenched, her eyes boring into my father's scalp.

My parents didn't speak. Sometimes, my mother chewed at her bottom lip. Other times, she craned her neck toward the television, watched it for a minute or two, then faced my father again. Twice, she pitched forward, mouth opening, hand stretching across the cushions toward my father's thigh before abruptly drawing up short and settling back on her end of the couch. My father stared at the noiseless television. Every so often, he blinked. Once, he cleared his throat then coughed.

Eventually, in a low, soothing tone, my mother said, "Frank, what happened to the girls?"

Waiting, I breathed slowly, scooping up the tiny background smells of my sister: chocolate chip cookies in a paper towel on her lap, cherry bubble gum from her mouth, something sharp and citrusy spilling off her hair. Finally, my father said, "I don't know. One was in the barn and the other was in the woods."

"Doing what?"

"Marie was in Roxie's stall. Jolene was playing in a pile of leaves."

"Playing? At seven in the morning?"

My father closed his eyes and moaned so faintly I could scarcely hear it. "That's what it looked like."

"Marie says you were chasing her."

"I wasn't chasing anybody."

My mother winced. She curled her knees to her chest and wreathed her arms around her shins. "Frank, is it happening again? I need to know. Jolene said you had a gun."

My father slumped forward, elbows on his knees, forehead braced between his palms, and said, "Please. Please, Adele, don't let them take me away. I can't go away again."

My mother's face crumpled, the corners of her lips turning downward, her bottom lip trembling. "You scared the girls."

"I didn't mean to."

Jolie snorted a warm breath through the slats of the grate. Her eyes were hard, and her mouth was a tight, thin line.

Downstairs, my mother's voice took on a fine edge. "Where's the gun now?"

"I wouldn't've hurt them."

"I know, but you have to give me the gun."

"I need that gun for protection."

"There's nobody to protect against, Frank."

"You don't understand." My father motioned vaguely toward the television screen and the puffs of smoke as American airplanes bombed some unseen enemy. "I need to have that gun with me. I don't feel safe without it. There's a war on."

"That's a different war. It's far away, not here in America. Not here on this farm."

"Korea was a long ways off."

"I'm scared for them," my mother said.

"But it still came home."

"I'm scared for you."

"Came home inside all of us." He sagged into the cushions and yanked my mother's hand against the meat of his right hip. "Used to be bone in there. Metal making up your skeleton, that ain't a thing you forget."

My mother drew her hand away and let it fall in her lap. "No, I don't suppose so. But you have to move on, Frank. It's been years. You've got me now. You've got kids now. You're safe with us. You don't need a gun."

My father swung his chin back and forth — no, no, no — as he said, "There's few things I ask of you, Adele. But that gun? I *need* that gun."

My mother smiled sadly. Her glance flicked from him to the television and back again. Indecision cut lines through her brow. Upstairs, Jolie made soft popping noises with her bubble gum, and I whispered, "Choose us. Choose us." My mother said, "I can't, Frank. You'll hurt the girls or maybe yourself. Give me the gun. Let me keep you safe."

After a long time, my father whimpered, "It's in the cupboard behind the tea cups."

My mother patted his thigh, kissed his cheek, and said, "I'll get it then I'll make us some coffee." She half-stood then added, "It's going to be all right, Frank." After she left, my father plodded over to the television and eased up the volume. A voice reported the death toll so far then mentioned that the enemy soldiers in Vietnam, just like the ones in Korea, were also called gooks. My father's face blanched.

My insides tensed, and I murmured, "Is that it?"

Jolie moved over to her bed. She curled into a ball on top of the mattress and with a dull, feeble voice, said, "Sounds like it."

I slipped behind her, weaving my fingers through hers, and mumbled, "It wasn't the first time."

I watched the rise and fall of her chest, smelled the chocolate from the cookies still grasped tightly against her belly. Eventually, she said, "For what?"

"That Daddy held a gun to his head."

My sister bleated a soft, moaning noise.

"Today, though, he made *me* be the one to give him a reason to live," I whispered. "When I was six, he came into the barn when I was playing in the hayloft, and he talked real soft to the horses. He put that gun to his head and asked them, 'Why shouldn't I pull the trigger? Just what do I got to live for?' He went horse to horse with his face all hard and mad, asking the same thing. When he got to the end of the line, he just left, and I was up there with my dolls watching the whole thing." My left temple started to throb. "Daddy had that same look today, all hard and mad. The difference was he had it while he was looking at me. He told me to sing a song or else he'd kill himself."

Moonlight glimmered through the window, blazing a silver band across my sister's cheek. Staring at the wall, her eyes flat and dull, she murmured, "What did you sing?"

"*This Little Light of Mine.*"

The heat between us cooled, and I reached for the comforter heaped at the foot of the bed. I heard my sister say faintly, "He hit me with the back of his hand. His wedding ring caught the side of my mouth."

Outside, the moonvine on the trellis sensed the darkness, and its wide, white flowers opened. My stomach muscles tightened and anger flared through me. "Did you tell Mama?"

She squeezed her eyes shut and ground her teeth together. Again, she bleated that soft, moaning noise.

I pulled her tightly to me and felt the nubs of her spine prodding into my belly. "It's going to be okay, Jolie. Let's go to sleep now. We won't change things by talking."

SOMETIMES, IN THE late afternoons, I would think about my little sister and ache. It was me who planted that seed, the one that took root in Jolene and convinced her that words held no hope. Over the years that seed sprouted and put forth leaves, blooming but bearing bad fruit. Long after I'd moved away, I understood it was *then*, in her bed, my mouth so close to her ear, her body trembling against mine, that Jolene decided to do what she did.

May 1966

AT THE FRONT edge of the yard, just beyond the gravel courtyard and a gentle slope of grass, an apple tree threw shade across a small mound of dirt. There, beneath a bough studded with pink blooms, Jolie stung my biceps with a stick she'd whittled to a point, and a bubble of blood welled up then oozed across my skin. I yelped and flailed backward, my heel smacking the round swell of a dying dandelion, scattering white spores across the lawn.

"He's buried there, I heard Daddy say." Jolie aimed the bloodied stick at the mound. "He was born dead, and Daddy buried him there."

I molded my palms to my narrow hips. "There's no other kids. How come you got to lie all the time?"

"It's my nature." She edged the toe of her old sneaker into the dirt. Quieter, she added, "Least that's what Daddy says."

"If somebody was buried there, there'd be a cross or a stone or something."

She shrugged, her thin shoulders hunching and the bones jutting up beneath the blue T-shirt she wore. "Daddy said they made one out of two sticks tied in the middle with twine. He said they planted it in the ground right after, but it got blown away when the wind kicked up and nobody's seen it since."

I rolled my eyes and snorted. "Well, why didn't they put out another one then?"

" 'Cause Daddy said he wanted to forget."

"How come you know all that?"

My little sister dropped the stick to the ground, and my blood spattered the grass. "Daddy talks late at night. He thinks he's all alone up in the attic. But there's a good hiding spot in the corner by Mama's busted sewing mannequin. I watch him sit by that footlocker and shuffle through the pictures in it like playing cards. I listen to him jabber on about the war and dead kids and how much he wishes things was different."

My face prickled, blood flooding my cheeks. I leaned my head toward hers and whispered, "What else did he say?"

"He's got a picture he talks to. He told it he was sorry its heart never beat outside Mama's belly, sorry that it never even got to take one breath. He says the worst sound he ever heard was the silence when there should've been a cry. He says he don't think he'll ever stop hearing it."

She knelt, pulling me down with her. "Daddy left that picture out once. It was a baby with his skin all wrinkled and pale. He had a stork bite like we both had when we were born." She brushed her fingers across the center of her forehead where her birthmark had been. "His eyes were shut, his mouth was cracked open, and his little round face looked just like Daddy's."

I heard the faintest click of a door hinge carried by the wind. I half-turned and caught my father's shape lumbering big and dark alongside the house then across the grass, eyes on us, fingers curled in a fist. Jolene didn't hesitate; she bolted for the woods beyond the hay field. He glowered after her for a moment then his eyes shifted back to me. When my father's black work boots stopped inches from my lap, I craned my neck, squinting upward in the sunlight, and noticed his face smeared with car grease and his eyes, hard and dull, glaring at me.

He squatted down, snatched my wrist, and panted the thick, sweet smell of clove cigarettes across my face. "What're you doing messing around out here?"

"Nothing. I—"

His face flushed, his grip clammy, my father jumped up and started to drag me toward the house. Inside me a tiny flare went up, a warning from my gut, and I shoved my heels into the soft ground, casting dents where, later, when a cool rain began to fall, water would pool. He yanked harder, his boots clipping my shins as I fought behind him, jerking like a fish on a hook. We tramped past the porch and alongside the house to the cellar. He hauled and I twisted, my leg muscles burning, my wrist aching. I stared at his broad back, remembering just last night when I'd pranced my fingers across his shoulder blades, and he'd shivered and laughed. He had hugged me, whispering in my ear, "You're pretty, you know that?"

"Daddy, please. You're hurting me."

The thin sound of my words broke his stride. He pivoted and leveled his eyes at me. "When you gonna learn a thing? That place is off limits. The C-O told you so."

"C-O?" I said, my voice shaking.

"C-O." He stared at the blankness of my face. "The commanding officer, for Godsakes. Orders is orders."

"I'm sorry," I shouted. "I'm sorry."

"That's why we got the brig," he said. "Don't you understand? You don't listen to orders, you end up dead. Or worse, somebody else ends up dead 'cause of you."

We trampled the grass, blades of it staining the white fabric of my sneakers. Closer to the cellar, he mumbled, "Ain't nobody respects the dead."

In the window above the kitchen sink, I caught sight of my mother's face and yelled, "Mama!"

She had her eyes pinned on us. I watched her face tighten then her body turning and her hair bouncing before she vanished into the dark of the house.

We stopped next to the cellar doors, and my father yelled, "Aw, Christ! Where's the M-P?" His eyes darted through the oak scrub dotting the base of the house. Finding no one, he said, "Hell, if you don't got to do everything yourself."

He released me then pulled a brown belt from the loops of his jeans. With one hand, he scooped up the ends so the rawhide made a whipping strap. I took a step back, then two. With the other hand, he heaved open a cellar door and pointed down the stairs. "Get in there and don't give me a hard time. I got to go after the one that was with you."

I had stepped on the top stair when my mother showed up, hurtling across the lawn, hollering, "Frank, what're you doing?"

His back to her, my father answered, "They got to learn."

My mother stopped on the grass next to my father, her chest heaving and flour sifting off her apron. She smelled of carrots and butter as she asked, "What's going on?"

"They got to learn," my father said again.

My mother looked between me, the belt, and my father's face. "Learn what?"

"They got to learn they can't disobey," my father muttered. "I found them under the apple tree. They ain't allowed around the apple tree."

"Is that true?" my mother asked me.

My head wobbled yes.

She sighed. "All right, Frank. They made a mistake. Let's go on in the house."

"No!" He shook his fist at my mother. "They got to learn. They got to listen the first time."

"What do you want them to do?" my mother said.

"Punishment's down there." He jabbed a finger toward the blackness beyond the cellar door. "They got to stay there till I say different."

"Don't you think that's harsh?"

"Harsh? Harsh is me doing nothing when they ain't listening. Harsh is letting somebody die."

My mother's head rocked backward, her eyes widened, and her demeanor changed. She said in a quiet, low voice, "Okay, Frank. All right." She reached over and squeezed my hand. "Go on, Ann Marie. Go down there, and we'll come get you soon." I opened my mouth to protest, but she said, "Now, Ann Marie, please."

My foot cleared the last step, and I stood on a small patch of swept dirt at the bottom, staring up at my mother and the weak smile on her face. Then the cellar doors banged shut, and the light went from a bright square to a thin blade. There was the scrape of steel as my father slid the bolt and locked me in. Afterward, I heard my mother's voice, "Where are you going?" And my father's answer, "The other one ran off. I got to find them."

Darkness flooded my eyes and ears and nose and mouth. I started to count — *one Mississippi, two Mississippi* — while I waited for my vision to adjust. Soon, the black shadows near the ceiling transformed into roots hung to dry. The hulking shapes against the far wall became metal shelves with mason jars full of peaches, tomatoes, and jam. I breathed in the smell of dirt from the floor, wax around the jar lids, lime to keep the mold down, and something sweet, too, like licorice and peppermint.

I took a step forward and noticed figures low to the ground, swaying lightly from my movement and then becoming still. I leaned down, and they swished around me, paper bodies making tiny scratching noises against my bare arms. This close, I could see a tulip fashioned from red construction paper, a hole stabbed in one petal and fishing line threaded through it. Eyes scanning, I counted more than fifty paper flowers — tulips, roses, daffodils. With some, I could look and tell what flower it was. With others, I had to boost their stems into the shaft of light and read the backward-slanting script that named them. I crumpled a rose in my fist, and when I released my fingers, the paper unfolded little by little. That day had been my first in the cellar as punishment, but I wondered, as dust swam along the edge of the sunlight, just how many trips it must've been for Jolene to churn out such a garden.

Outside in the woods beyond the fields, my father squatted on a fallen log and dragged Jolie across his knee. He bared her bottom and she tried to shield her backside with her hands, but my father swatted them away. He brought the leather down, the flat edge cutting into her naked skin. Jolie's eyes clouded, her face pinched up, and I heard, however faintly, the scream that broke from her mouth. With my fingernails, I sliced furrows into the dirt of the wall. That little pebble in my gut, the place where I housed my rage, fattened.

I started to mouth numbers, losing track a few times, beginning again with a number I'd already uttered, and as the cellar door swung open, I whispered, *Two-twelve Mississippi.* Jolene cowered beside my father, his hand wrenching her arm. Her hair was filled with dirt, her shorts bloodied in back, her face red and splotchy. My father shoved her toward the stairs and said, "You two are gonna stay down there till you learn to listen. Orders is orders."

"I'm sorry, Daddy," I hollered.

"Sorry? Sorry don't mean nothing." He started to rethread the belt through the loops of his jeans. "Sorry'll just get you killed."

"Uh-huh," I said.

Head down, Jolie reached the dirt floor and moved into the shadows. My father slammed the cellar door, tiny slivers of wood showering down the stairs, and threw the bolt. With a low, growling sound, I heard my sister's voice come from the darkness, saying, "You sonofabitch."

Seeing only the faint outline of her in the dimness, I said softly, "You shouldn't swear, 'specially not at Daddy."

Her voice came back hard and flat. "You sound like Mama. Now all you got to say is, '*Vulgarity is the lack of vocabulary,*' and you'd be her."

"He's our daddy."

"He's a bastard." She scooped a handful of dirt in her hand, splayed her fingers and watched it sift to her feet. "That's the last time he gets to hear me holler." Softer, she added, "That's the last time I'm gonna beg."

She shuffled along the wall, touching it as a guide, to the corner near the canning shelves. There was a spark of flint, the smell of sulfur, and then a soft popping noise as she lit a propane lantern. Light filled the room, and I could see my sister crouched beside a cardboard box, her hands digging through it. I could also make out the edges of the flowers, the paper curled from the dampness of the floor. A hard little lump raised itself in my throat.

"How long you been coming down here?" I asked.

The shuffling stopped. Jolie rocked back on her haunches and popped a peppermint candy into her mouth. "This is where he always puts me."

"But why?"

"Mama says I remind him of himself. She says we're just too much alike."

Stunned, I said, "You talked to Mama about this?"

But Jolie didn't answer that question. Instead, her voice slipped a notch lower and she said, "But I think it's 'cause I made a place where he can't touch me. I got somewhere that he can't ever go." She tapped a finger to her temple. "I got a whole world right up in here, and he can't ever get there." Jolie motioned with a wide sweep of her arm, first toward the ceiling and the flowers hanging down then to the wall and dozens of papers pinned to the dirt. "The flowers and the drawings are just part of what's in my head. He can't touch that place in me, and *that's* what he don't like."

"How do you know that?"

She shrugged and plunged her hands again into the box. "I feel it in my gut. I know it's true."

I moved within a few feet of Jolene, stopped, and said, "He was talking about a brig."

Her hands flew as she searched, tossing paper, markers, and ribbons out of the box and onto the floor. Her back to me, she answered, "He says that a lot."

"What's a brig?"

"Someplace to put somebody, I guess."

"Why's he got to put us any place?"

"Why's he point a gun at his head and make you sing?"

"I don't know."

"He's crazy, that's why." Suddenly, she stilled. "Hah! She left it."

I crouched beside her and said, "What?"

Smiling, Jolie thrust a dull metal object toward my face. "Mama left me a hole punch."

"Hole punch?"

"I asked, and she left it."

"Asked?"

My blank look forced a snort from Jolene. "One day Mama left me a note saying I should write down whatever I needed and she'd get it. So I just scribble a list and plunk it on the kitchen counter. The next time Daddy drags me down here, the thing I asked for's in the box."

My gut tightened. "But how come she doesn't just stop him from hauling you down here in the first place?"

Jolie pocketed the hole punch and rifled through the glitter, felt, and beads that ringed the ground around her. "Don't really matter. Long as I got what I need, I can keep myself busy. She said it'd be easier this way."

I felt light-headed as I said, "Easier?"

My sister plucked items from the dirt and dusted them off. Her voice was fluid, easy. "Besides, usually, he don't hurt me. Usually, he just lugs me down here and forgets me for a few hours."

"How long's he been doing that?"

She cut her eyes to me then to the ground. She gnawed on her bottom lip as she ticked off the time with nods of her chin. "Two or three years, about."

My mouth made a sudden oval. I hadn't been expecting years. "Doesn't it make you mad that Mama doesn't do a thing?"

"She brings me the stuff I need." With a quiet sound, she cleared her throat. "She gave me this." Jolie dug in the front pocket of her shorts and pulled out a round seed, tiny as a sweet pea. "She said faith as small as a mustard seed could move mountains."

"That's not a mustard seed."

"I know. Mama said mustard seeds are so tiny you can't hardly see them. She said she wanted me to have something I could hold. I don't even know what plant this seed makes when it's grown. But it's small enough, and that's more than enough faith to make things different."

Jolene tipped her cupped palm, and the seed fell into my hand. I ran my finger along its smooth, brown skin and said, "Where'd you hear that?"

"Mama's Bible says, *If you have faith as small as a mustard seed, you can say to this mountain, Move from here to there and it will move. Nothing will be impossible for you.*"

I envisioned dirt and rocks and tree roots twisting and splintering, shattering into tiny pieces then reforming somewhere else. I thought, *if that can happen, maybe God can make my father all right again.* Maybe God could take my father and move him back in time, back to the person he was before 1961 when John F. Kennedy was inaugurated and of Vietnam said, "we shall pay any price ... to insure the survival and the success of liberty." Before those words, my father smiled easily. He carted us on his shoulders. He laughed way down in his belly. He danced us around the living room on top of his toes. In my throat welled up an ache a hundred times the size of that seed.

Jolie plucked the seed from my hand and pushed it back into her pocket. She said, "You need anything?"

I thought, *I need Daddy back the way he was. I need a miracle.* Out loud, my voice quavering, I said, "Some paper. A big piece of it."

She reached for a yard-long cylinder leaning upright against the wall. "I got a tube of brown package wrap right here."

I sculpted a map of my future life that day. In the supply box, I discovered little trinkets — a photograph of Jolie and me, a dried pink rose petal, a silver locket with a busted hinge so its miniature round door hung cockeyed. I found a stack of faded magazines on the ground, then a puckered Sears catalog, and finally a dozen or so yellowed, dusty newspapers. I lined these things around me then sliced a wide swatch of brown paper from the roll. I weighted the corners with mason jars stuffed with peaches then picked up a thick black marker.

With ink bleeding into the paper, I printed in large, careful block letters, WHO I WILL BE. I rooted around for a blue crayon and framed my declaration with lopsided stars. From the newspaper, I clipped a smiling woman in a light taffeta gown grasping the hand of a man in a dark satin waistcoat. I pasted them to my map and wrote underneath, A MAN WHO LOVES ME. I rubbed the woman's face with my thumb, the newsprint eroding and the brown-paper backing showing through. With scissors that left a scalloped edge, I cut my head from the photograph of Jolene and me then glued it above the woman's graceful neck.

The stack of magazines near my feet bore children, expensive cars, and big, beautiful houses; the Sears catalog diamond rings, brand new furniture, and porcelain dolls. I scrambled through my markers again, sending a green one across the floor and into the canning shelves with a soft *thunk*. Underneath every image, I scrawled the words about who I would be in the future. Under the cars, I printed: I WILL

HAVE SOMEONE TO DRIVE ME; the house: SO BIG THAT THERE WILL ALWAYS BE PLACES TO HIDE; the diamond ring: SEVEN CARATS; the furniture: NO MORE RICKETY BED FRAMES THAT CREAK EVERY TIME I MOVE; the dolls: A COMPLETE COLLECTION, NOT JUST THE ONES WE CAN AFFORD. Finally, under the pasted children, their paper bodies smeared and wrinkled, I wrote: I WILL BE A <u>GOOD</u> MOTHER. <u>MY</u> CHILDREN WILL LOVE ME.

After I formed the last letter, I glanced up to see Jolie with a giant pad of paper in her lap. The black marker in her right hand circled furiously, sketching our father as a stick figure. Her fingers slowed then stopped, pressing down hard so the ink seeped into the grain and formed two enormous, spreading stains for eyes. Afterward, her hand jerked up and down, making jack-o-lantern teeth, sharp and pointed. Her left hand started to whirl, a brown marker looping a belt in my father's stick hand. She paused, blew the bangs from her eyes, and scanned the ground for a yellow crayon to slash out an image of herself, a stick figure limp as an unstuffed cushion, slung over my father's knee, staring into the dirt, X's where her eyes should've been. Without looking up, she said, "Do you think faith will save us?"

"I don't know."

"Sometimes I think so. Sometimes not. It's such a small thing." She grabbed the black marker again. Her wrist jerked back and forth, blotching out our father's oval face, his eyes smudging into his ears, into the sky, off the edge of the page, and into the meaty part of her thumb. "And he's so big."

I hunched over my map, pasting red beads like holly berries to the paper. Instead of answering her, I counted the beads that studded my future life. As I reached fifty-eight, Jolie murmured, "Do you think God keeps score?"

"Like a game?"

"Like if we do something that's a sin, then God has Daddy punish us? Like if you do something bad, something bad happens to you?"

I stared at my map, glistening with wants and hopes and dreams. "I don't think so."

Jolie crinkled the edge of her picture then, with a small yank of her arm, tore the entire sheet of paper from its pad. "Is that why this is happening?"

"Daddy's sick," I mumbled without thinking, tipping my palm so the beads I held pooled in the dirt. "He has to take his medicine is all."

A month before, I had gone searching for a roll of toilet paper in my parents' bathroom and found instead a wall of prescription bottles with my father's name on each of them. I picked up one after another, reading: Lithium, Stelizine, Mellaril, Compazine, Haldol. Years later, I would pick up a Physician's Desk Reference and find out my father was doped up on anti-depressants, heavy-duty tranquilizers, and anti-nausea pills. I would find out that all had side effects, some incredibly severe, and most had stringent dietary requirements in order for them to work properly. Back then, though, I only knew there were a lot of bottles. I was so focused, I didn't hear the footsteps padding across the carpet. It was only the smell of perfume, something flowery and sweet, that made me turn to see my mother staring back at me, her cheeks shedding their color, her eyes flaring wide at the bottle clasped in my hand.

"I was ..." I said. "I mean ... I wasn't snooping. I just wanted some toilet paper."

A sad look settled itself on her face. She sighed and took the bottle from me. "It was just a matter of time before somebody found out." She knelt beside me, returning the bottle to the others and shutting the cabinet door. "Please don't tell anyone, Ann Marie. Daddy's sick. He's not been right since Korea. You know he fought a war in Korea, don't you?"

I nodded.

"He got better for a while, the medicines seemed to work. But ever since this country committed to Vietnam, he's been worse again. All the reports on TV and in the papers just seem to make him sicker." My mother tilted her face toward the window, and dusty yellow light fell across her skin. "He's got a scar from the top of his hip to the middle of his thigh. He got sent home because of that. He nearly got killed over there."

"But what's the matter with him now?"

She cupped her palm to my cheek and stroked my skin. "I'm sorry you have to know this. You're so young." She smiled gently and said, "The doctor called it schizophrenia. Your daddy doesn't remember things the way he used to. Sometimes he thinks things aren't what they are. Yesterday he flung a pencil across the room. He thought it was a bug, a walking stick. Do you understand?"

My head dipped toward my chest, and I stared at the floor. Quietly, I said, "Sometimes he doesn't know who me and Jolie are. Sometimes he calls us soldiers. Sometimes he calls us *mama-san*."

My mother moved her hand from my cheek to my chin and pushed upward, guiding me to look her in the eye. "You listen to me. If he ever does that again, you keep telling him over and over again who you are. Say, 'Daddy, I'm Ann Marie.' Do you understand?"

Her words felt like a thousand pinpricks against my skin. I didn't want to know this truth, so I looked toward the window and a Monarch butterfly circling slowly around the milkweed in the flowerbed.

She said again, "Do you understand?"

"Uh-huh."

She released me and rose slowly to her feet. "I have to put dinner on. Daddy's a little sick, that's all. I'll take him to the doctor again and get stronger medicine. Please don't say anything to anybody." She paused then added, "Including Jolene. People around this town talk enough as it is."

Something hard and tight plugged my gut. Anger, maybe. Fear, yes. Mostly, though, it was the thoughts — *Why him? Why us?* — wheedling their way in.

In the coolness of the cellar, Jolie stood up and said, "What?"

Pushing beads along the dirt, I answered loudly, "I don't think God keeps score."

"If He did," she muttered on her tiptoes, her thin arms raising the blackened picture of our father against the wall, her narrow fingers sticking pushpins in its corners, "it looks like we're losing." She stepped back, admired her work, then asked, "You done?"

Poring over my swatch of brown paper, I counted three bare patches, each the size of my fist. "Nearly."

"Better hurry."

"Why?"

She glanced at the stairs. "Won't be long now. He'll be back."

"And then what?"

My little sister frowned. "Then nothing. We'll go back into the house. We'll act like nothing happened."

"Can't I take it with me? It's the map of my future."

"No. It has to stay. Everything has to stay."

"But why?"

"Because there's something down here that makes me feel good, and if you go and show what you made to somebody like Mama or Daddy, you'll bust the spell around this place and around me. Then the magic'll get sucked right out of here, and this place'll be nothing but the stinky, old cellar again."

I smeared a thin layer of glue across each of the bare spots on my map then raked up whatever was within reach — pink feathers, gold glitter, brown leaves, silver yarn, black stones — and poured it on top. I blew a few hot breaths then waved my hands over top, trying to dry the glue. I hauled my swatch of brown paper to the wall and fastened it beneath her drawing. She handed me a purple marker and said, "You have to sign it. All artists have to sign their work."

I scratched my name on the bottom. Jolene gnawed on a strand of black licorice while she walked to the edge of her flower garden near the stairs.

"Is my map straight?" I said.

"That don't matter. What matters is something stuck inside you is out now, and it's too late for him to stop it."

At that moment, I understood that every last thing in Jolene's drawings — the curve of a nose, the glint in an eye — held significance for her. I studied my feet while a bad feeling started to swim through me. In a hurry to fill up the blank spaces, I had dumped any old thing onto the map of my future life. I opened my mouth to tell Jolene that I needed to redo my map, but her head was cranked toward the stairs, eyes staring up the shaft. The wood rattled and sunlight blazed down, enveloping my sister like a halo. My father hollered, "All right. Time's up." Then he turned and lumbered away.

"It's over, Marie," Jolie blurted, her voice gone flat, her breath swishing the fishing line of a blue paper tulip. "At least for today."

July 1967

OUTSIDE, THE AIR was thick with the smells of barbequed beef and fried chicken, lemonade, potato salad, baked beans, and the ripe, soft rind of a melon. At the picnic table behind our house, my father sprawled his legs underneath the wood planks and faced the fields, wheat bending low in the breeze. He'd gotten slow in the last few months: his movements hitching and jerking like a marionette. Suddenly, he half-turned to stare towards the front yard at the apple tree whose branches dropped soft, rotted fruit onto the grass. He grunted a low, "Huh." I sat next to him, following his gaze to a blue jay pecking at the ground beneath the tree.

"They got eyes, you know?" he said to no one in particular.

"What, Daddy?" I said.

Jolene sat across the table, flicking her gaze between our father and me while she drummed her fingers against the table.

"Eyes. The dead got eyes." He faced me and huffed a warm, moist breath across my face. "I seen 'em."

"Oh," I said.

"Maybe they can't see, but they got eyes. Eyes that some animal can feed on." Panic laced his voice and he lashed out, gripping my shoulders. "Promise me that ain't gonna happen to me."

I stiffened and barked, "I promise, Daddy."

"I seen too much of that. I ain't gonna go that way."

Jolene pounded louder, fingernails crashing against the wood. My father sighed and shifted his focus to the wheat stalks fluttering in the wind. He leaned forward, staring intently like he expected somebody to come walking out between the rows.

Jolene stopped thumping and jerked a finger to her temple. She wound it in a slow circle while she mouthed the word *crazy*. An image of her like that, eyes narrowed, mouth agape, ridiculing our father, even though I knew it was true, lodged itself in the knot in my belly where I would remember it forever. Jolene dropped her hand back to the table, waited a beat, then started thrumming again. After a while, she said, "Here comes Mama."

My mother sashayed down the small slope from the house, a plate of raw burgers in one hand and a bottle of ketchup in the other. The wind caught the hem of her dress and then her apron. It blew hair into her mouth, and she sputtered and spit, angling her face so the breeze would blow it back out. She moved toward us that way, with her body facing and her head turned away. When she reached the picnic table, she dropped the food and dipped her fingers into her apron pocket for a black elastic band she used to tie her hair in a ponytail.

"It's windy out here," she said. "Not good for a picnic." She plopped the meat on the grill then added, "Jolene, stop it. That sound's going to drive me crazy."

Jolie's fingers stilled. Her eyes narrow slits, she glowered at our father then blurted, "Daddy, do you love us?"

My father reached up and yanked the baseball cap he'd been wearing off his head. He beat the stiff brim of it against his thigh as he peered at the wheat, eyes squinting, trying to see something that wasn't there.

My mother poked at the burgers with the tines of a fork and said, "Lord have mercy, of course he does."

"How come he never says it?"

"Hush!"

"Well, how come?"

"Frank," my mother said in a low tone.

My father flinched at her voice. He craned his neck toward the grill. "Huh?"

Slowly, my mother said, "Do ... you ... love ... Jolene?"

My father glanced at Jolene then back to my mother. "Course I do. She's my daughter."

"How come you never say it?" my sister spat.

"Jolene!" my mother said. "That's enough."

"I want to know."

My father studied the cap folded between his hands. His sweat had stained an oblong patch in the red band. He traced the blotch with a fingernail while his face pinched up like a man who'd just been slapped. His bottom lip quivered, and he bit into it to still it.

My mother, her eyes on Jolene, said, "Your daddy's got other ways of showing you he loves you. That tree house he built you? That space he cleared in the woods? The rocks he dragged so you'd have a place to build a fire? He did all that because he loves you."

Jolene's cheeks flushed. She waved vaguely in the direction of our father and, her voice barely above a whisper, said, "Well, how come he don't say it? Missy Waylan's daddy always tells her he loves her."

"People are just different, Jolene. Not everybody shows love in the same way."

"I just want to hear him say it, is all."

My father twisted the fabric in his hand, the eyelets stretching and puckering like mouths. "I love you, Jolene," he said thickly. "You too, Ann Marie. I'm sorry it has to be like this. I'm the sorriest one of all."

Those words set my scalp to tingling, and I threaded my arm through his. "It's okay, Daddy."

"You too, Adele," my father murmured.

"I know, Frank." To Jolene, she said, "Now that everything's said, can we get back to our picnic?"

The burgers charred. Jolene buried her face in a slice of watermelon and juice ran down her chin and neck, staining the collar of her T-shirt. She spit the seeds in the grass, where, by the end of summer, two would have rooted and grown fruit. My mother popped her fingers in and out of her mouth, licking off ketchup and crumbs. I speared baked beans with the tines of my fork while my father sipped at a glass of lemonade.

After a while, my father sighed loudly. "Jolene, how about after lunch we play a round of tag? Loser buys cones for everybody at Bill's in town."

Her mouth hovering above the melon's meat, Jolene said, "I ain't got any money."

"You got a whole dented Folger's can full of change in the basement," I said.

She shot a nasty look in my direction. To my mother, she said, "Can Patrick come?"

"Who?" my father asked.

"The little red-headed boy down the road," my mother said, smoothing her hands along her apron.

My father plunked his drink on the table, and the ice cubes clinked against the glass. "The one who rides his bike in front of our house and won't ever come up the driveway?"

"Yes, that's him."

"Can he come?" Jolene whined.

"Why don't he ever come up the drive?"

"Shy, maybe," my mother said.

"Way he acts, you'd think he was afraid of us."

A dark look crossed my mother's face. It wasn't lost on me that fewer and fewer people had been coming around of late. Whether my mother didn't invite them or they just politely offered excuses not to stop by, I didn't know. Except driving past in his cruiser, waving one sunburned arm out the window, the sheriff, Ned Horner, a man my parents grew up with, never saw us. The people my parents had surrounded themselves with for so long — playing rummy out on the porch late at night, sipping cheap apple wine from mason jars, throwing dull-tipped darts at the corkboard in the basement — were suddenly quite absent.

Other people still brought their cars to my father for repairs because he was the cheapest, honest mechanic around. They were customers, though, not people who cared about our family. I thought about asking where everybody was. I wanted to know when Ned would reappear with a handful of taffy. But when I glanced at my mother, at the strain on her face, I said nothing. My mother often paused before she spoke, and I wondered if, in those silent moments, she was sorting through the truth, searching for a place where she could bend it into a plausible lie. She pumped up her smile and spooned potato salad onto my father's plate. Finally, she said, "Patrick's just young."

My father bit off a hunk of burger and ketchup fell from the bun, splattering onto the table. He prodded at the spot with one finger and red clung to his skin. A thin, whining noise broke from his throat, and he snapped his wrist over and over, trying to get the ketchup off.

My mother grabbed a napkin, spit on it, and said, "Here, Frank, I'll get that. It's just ketchup."

My father groaned.

Jolie said, "Well, can he come?"

My father stared at his finger then at the table where the ketchup had been. The wood held a dark ragged stain and a tuft of torn napkin. He closed his eyes, waited, opened them again. He said, "How old is he?"

"My age. Ten. Can he go?"

"Why won't he come to the house?"

No one answered him. My mother nibbled at a cob of corn; Jolene bounced her feet underneath the table; I mashed baked beans into my plate. Eventually, my father said, "All right, he can go."

My mother exhaled loudly. The subject had been abandoned, and the answer — *He is afraid; he's scared of you* — remained buried where, at least for that day, it wouldn't have to be spoken out loud. A smile turned the corners of my mother's mouth, and she flapped a hand in my father's direction. "Lord, you wonder why these kids have no manners. Frank, don't talk with your mouth full."

SHRIEKING AND LAUGHING, Jolie hurtled across the front lawn toward the buckeye tree, its one side blooming thick cones of white flowers, and flattened herself against its black bark. "Safe!" she yelled. "The buckeye's safe."

My father, who was never very fast but of late had gotten slow then slower, lumbered behind her, huffing and pinching at a stitch in his side. A dozen yards or so from the tree, he stopped and curled over his knees. My mother and I sat on the porch steps, her one stair above me, while we watched his lips move. Right then, we couldn't hear what he was saying. Much later, in the darkness of the kitchen pantry, I would learn that he was muttering, " 'It's survival of the fittest,' the sarge said. 'You ain't fit, you don't survive.' "

Jolie yelled, "You give up, Daddy?"

"I got to get my breath back," he said.

"Buckeye's safe!"

He fell to one knee, cradling his forehead in his palm. My mother stood up, raised a hand to shade her eyes, and said loudly, "Everything all right, Frank?"

"Fine. Leave me be. I'm fine."

My father felt her stare piercing him like so many sharp needles, and he knew, however obscurely in his head, that if he didn't say something normal, my mother would swamp him with questions. From his crouched position, he hollered toward Jolene, "You ain't allowed to hang onto that branch all day."

Her feet dangling just above the ground, Jolene yelled, "Why not?"

"Rules say you got a minute and then you got to let go."

"What rules?"

"My rules."

My mother's shoulders eased, her face relaxed. She sat back down behind me and pulled a brown rattail comb and a handful of skinny black elastic bands from her apron pocket. She wove her fingers through my hair, the tail end of the comb lifting and separating, her thin fingers braiding strands into a wide, loose plait. After a time, she started humming a slow country tune, and the rhythm of her fingers and her voice made my head lull forward and my eyelids slide half-closed.

"George Jones?" I muttered.

"Yes."

"What song?"

"*Color of the Blues*. It's one of my favorites."

"You could be a singer."

"A long time ago, maybe." Her voice faltered. "Not now."

I perked up, turning my head to talk over my shoulder. "You could go to Nashville and be a star."

"Stay still," she said, cupping my ears and moving my head to where it had been. The comb whisked through my hair, and her fingers brushed against my scalp. "I'm happy here. This is where I am."

"You don't have to be."

She glimpsed at my father's back as he plodded toward Jolene. Softly, she said, "When you have babies, you'll understand. Things change. That's just the way it is."

We stayed quiet for a time, her braiding my hair, me staring at the whitewashed wood between my feet. After a few minutes, she started humming another song in low tones.

"Who sings that?" I asked.

"That's one I wrote."

"Will you sing it for me?"

"I just have the music. No words yet."

She gathered up my hair, drawing it away from my neck, and her warm, moist breath stippled my skin. Across the horizon, Jolene's legs were pumping toward the pond, down a slope just south of the buckeye tree. Soon enough, she was stumbling then falling, her heel sliding along some dew-slicked grass. My father barged toward her with his face ruddy and his cheeks puffing and deflating like balloons.

"Gotcha!" he said, grabbing her arm. For a second, fear darted across Jolene's face. It darted across my father's, too. This girl he'd caught, her eyes wide and white, her bones small and thin, her face crumpled, eyebrows slanted down, teeth bared, transported him to an old place, a place he tried hard not to go.

"Daddy, you're squeezing too tight."

Jolene jerked her arm away. My father stared at her for a nearly a minute before stammering, "I win. You're buying."

She stood up, the pinched look fading from her face. She dusted herself off and shouted toward my mother and me, "I ain't got any money, no matter what Marie says."

On the porch stairs, I sat with my elbows braced against my knees, my chin sunk in the valley of my palms, and my eyes fluttering open and shut. What I said next, I hadn't meant to say out loud. I whispered, "How come he don't like us?"

The pointed end of the comb dug into my scalp then my mother pulled it away and held it against her breast. "He loves you. You're his flesh and blood."

Staring out across the front lawn, I said, "But he don't *like* us much, does he? Least it doesn't seem that way."

She smoothed her palm across the bumps of my woven hair. "They're peas in a pod, Jolene and your daddy. She's just like him, headstrong and stubborn. She says what's on her mind, and everybody else be damned. Your sister's not afraid of anything."

"She's afraid of Daddy," I said, watching my father trudge toward the buckeye tree while Jolene was nowhere to be seen. "I am, too."

My mother swooped an elastic band around the end of my braid and said softly, "He's sick."

"That don't make us less afraid of him."

Her voice dropped an octave lower. "He's your father. You have to listen to him, but you don't have to be afraid of him."

I watched my father stand beside the buckeye tree and rest a hand against its trunk. "Seems like he's happier when we're out of the way."

My mother laid the warm moistness of her palm on my shoulder. "The war made him somebody afraid all the time. I think he sees in you kids what life should've been, and it makes him sad. Makes him angry."

"But how come he's angry at us?"

I listened to her sigh then say, "Ann Marie, honey, he's not angry at you. Your daddy got taken away years ago to a war that nearly killed him. Now he just needs his family to love him. We just have to love him no matter what he does."

I leaned backward so my head pressed against her breast. I could feel her heart and with every beat, the hope I held tightly in my gut, the hope that she might come to my rescue, shriveled like a parched bean too long on the vine.

"What about us?" I whispered.

She wrapped her arms around me and said, "We can't be selfish now, Ann Marie. We've got to be strong."

I squeezed my eyes shut, breathed in and then out. "What happened to Daddy during the war?"

My mother shook her head slowly, the road dust churning into the bodies of my father's platoon, into her own stunned face when she saw him off the plane with a cane in his right hand and a hollowness in his eyes, into his sharp teeth and screaming mouth against her lap while she dug her fingers through the silk of his thick hair on the first night he was home.

"It was a long time ago."

"I'm twelve. I'm old enough."

She kissed the top of my head. "Honey, even I'm not old enough to know everything that happened to your daddy."

When I opened my eyes again, my father was patting his palm up and down the tree's bark. He repeatedly opened his mouth, waited a beat, then closed it again as if he were chatting with the branches. I asked, "What was he like before?"

My mother stroked the pale base of her throat. A small smile lit up her face. "He used to laugh a lot. He made me laugh so hard that my insides ached and my bladder threatened to let go. He chewed gum and worked on cars for a living, like he does now, but back then his face was all soft curves and freckles. Back then, his hands weren't all notched with scars. And there was always this smell in the air around him. Car grease, fried potatoes, and mint gum." Her soft tone turned raspy, and she tucked a strand of her hair behind her ear. "He was tall even then, with ropes of muscle. Lord, I used to flush when I saw him."

A breeze blew past us, and my mother's scent — thick, sweet, strawberry lotion — swelled in the air. When the stillness between us became an awkward thing, I said, "How come you never talk about the way Daddy used to be? Don't you miss him like that?"

The soft shadowy holes of my mother's nostrils flared wide, and she mumbled, "That's gone now." Something harsh sliced through her voice when she spoke again. "It was a long time ago. Your father doesn't need to be reminded of what isn't."

All those years ago, I didn't understand the nuance of conversation; I didn't read correctly the glint in her eyes, the stiffness of her back, the downward curve of her lips. So I asked, "But what about us? What about what we need?"

My mother, who had pledged herself to my father, sporting his class ring and giving him her virginity before he was shipped off to a war in Korea, was blindsided when he'd come home, a faint shadow of the man she'd remembered. It was too late to take back the words she'd uttered before he left, the ones where she promised to love him forever, and so she'd had no choice but to stay, her own mind thinking, *But what about me?* On the porch, resentment blazed in her, and she said, "Your father does the best he can. He puts a roof over your head and food on the table. If the best you can give back to him is ungrateful, spoiled selfishness, then I suggest you go on up to your room."

Her bitter face made my stomach wither into a hard pebble. "Mama, what's wrong?"

"Your daddy's had it rough. I had it rough. He saved me from my own mother and father, who came home drunk and spent all their money on booze so there was nothing for me or your uncles to eat. Your daddy took me away from all that, and I'm not leaving him. I'm not going back there. Do you understand me?" She slammed the flat of her hand against the porch so hard that in a half hour, there would be a plum-colored bruise on her palm. "I can't make it on my own."

All I wanted to do was make her stop talking before she said something she couldn't take back. "I didn't mean ..."

But my words were small and weak, and she brushed them aside with a wave of her hand. "When I look at him now, I can still see the person he used to be. *That's* the person I can't turn my back on." She rubbed at her injured hand and let her eyes wander over the horizon. Her gaze followed the gentle slope of the front lawn until it tumbled into the ditch near the road. She said in a quiet voice, "And I can't go back to being poor and having nothing. Second-hand clothes. Only a potato to eat. Please don't ask me to choose, Ann Marie. I'd have to choose him. I'd have to. Please don't force me to choose."

My face shattered under her declaration, the power of her words dwarfing all my little desires until I was left feeling small and unimportant. I poked the tip of my tongue between my lips as if I were tasting the phrase, *I'd have to choose him.*

My mother patted my back. "Don't cry, Ann Marie. It'll be hard for a while, but everything'll be all right. Why don't you go into the house and find Jolene? We'll head to town for ice cream."

As the screen door slammed shut behind me, I heard her say, "He's having a good day. We ought to be thankful he's having a good day."

In the kitchen, I plucked a knife with jagged, sharp teeth from the silverware drawer. I caught my reflection in the blade and frowned. Etched on my brain like tiny hatch marks was my mother's voice, *I'd have to choose him.* I wished broken bones on my mother and blindness on my father, but I knew, hence the shame and the frown, that I wouldn't really dare want them to come true.

Upstairs in my bedroom, I crouched beneath the window with my nose pressed against the pane. I watched my mother plod cowlike and slow toward the buckeye tree while sunlight slipped between the sheer curtains and landed in a square on the window frame. I crossed the room to my closet, found a small red pillow, and jammed the knife's serrated blade into it over and over, white batting spilling onto the floor, until my arm ached. Standing by as my father slid slowly away from me, as my mother was a silent and unhelpful witness, as my sister mirrored my own desperate need to be loved, as other families lived normal lives, I felt my gut, just above my pubic bone, tighten again.

My closet was fat with summer dresses and faded T-shirts as I climbed beneath them, my fingers parting the layers of fabric. Sweating and breathing hard, I lifted the metal blade and sliced one deep mark into the soft wood of the wall. A sliver fell to the carpet, and I rolled it between my fingers. Something about the feel of it calmed me, and so the next day and the next until I finally left home for good, I would stab the wall, carving out another notch, keeping a daily count of the years that remained.

AT A ROUND table near the window at Bill's Diner, Jolie sucked on a chocolate cone. Our neighbor, Patrick, a thin red-headed boy with a face full of freckles, curved his body beside hers. They leaned their heads together and spoke in hushed tones. Across from them, I sat on a ladderback chair next to my father and stirred the vanilla ice cream of a banana split until it dripped from the spoon. My mother wore her sunglasses on top of her head and waited at the counter, plucking napkin after napkin from a metal dispenser. The diner's owner, Bill, was stooped with age, his hair thinned, his glasses framing two of the weariest eyes I'd ever seen. A long time ago, he used to come to our house for supper.

He handed my mother some change and said something I couldn't hear. My mother smiled faintly then brushed the back of her hand underneath her eyes. Bill reached across the counter, mouthing *I'm sorry*, but my mother backed away, bumping into a woman in line behind her.

My mother said, "I'm sorry, I'm sorry," and hurried toward the bathroom in the back of the restaurant. Finding it in use, she leaned against the doorjamb and dabbed at her face with stiff paper napkins while she spat, "I'm sorry, you're sorry, Lord, *everybody's* sorry."

At our table, my father balanced a hot fudge sundae in a white paper cup between his hands. He grunted and moments later, his fingers danced wildly so that only two touched the cup at any one time. He narrowed his eyes and puckered his mouth, his tongue flicking out to wet his lips.

"You okay, Daddy?" I said.

Jolene and Patrick stopped whispering. My sister cut her eyes between our father and me while chocolate ice cream dripped from the bottom of her cone onto her jeans. A second later, she glanced toward the diner's front door, a few steps away.

"Shrapnel," my father said. "It's full of burning metal."

"Huh?" I said.

"There's not supposed to be metal in here."

"It's ice cream," I said. "A sundae."

"Sarge said not to touch any stray pieces. Said they might be burning." My father dropped the cup and it tipped on its side, spilling hot fudge and nuts across the table. "He said they might scorch our skin clean off."

Jolie jumped up so fast she knocked over the chair she'd been sitting in. While it clattered to the linoleum floor, she grabbed Patrick's sleeve, hauling him up and dragging him toward the exit. Over her shoulder, she yelled, "We're gonna get some air." The bell above the door tinkled as they went out.

"You hear that?" my father said.

"It's a bell, Daddy."

He shoved back from the table, chair legs screeching, as melted ice cream seeped toward him. By then, a few strangers at tables near us began to take notice — an older couple with sly glances, two little boys pointing us out to their mother.

"It's ice cream," I said again. "Please, Daddy, can't you see that it's just ice cream?"

"There's metal in it," he hollered, and a few more heads, including my mother's in the corner by the bathroom, turned to stare at us. My face burned hot. My father's sundae spread across the table. My mother clutched a wad of tiny napkins to her chest and hurried toward us.

"Frank, what's the matter? Is something wrong with the ice cream?"

My father's confusion increased with every pair of eyes boring into him. He bowed his head, pressing his fingers to his temples. "There's metal in it." He sighed hard. "It was ... I saw ... I don't know."

My mother mopped at the sundae, careful to scoot the mess away from my father. "Marie?"

"I don't know, Mama. He said something about the metal burning him."

Outside, Jolie and Patrick huddled together at a picnic table, their backs to us. My mother picked up the half-empty cup and righted it. Quietly, she said, "There doesn't look to be any metal, Frank."

My father moaned. Bill, who'd kept an eye on us since we came in, scurried out from behind the cash register with a wet rag in his hand. Standing behind my mother, he asked, "Everything all right?"

My mother startled at the sound of his voice. She stuffed the soiled napkins into the dessert cup and handed it to him. "Everything's fine, Bill. We shouldn't have come here." In a louder voice to benefit the people gawking at us, she said, "He's just overtired. Everything's fine."

At home, she tucked my father into bed in Jolie's room, pulled the shades, and closed the door softly behind her. She stared at the door for nearly a minute before her shoulders slumped and she covered her face with her hands. Jolie had gone off with Patrick, and it was just me, leaning against the hallway wall, watching my mother tremble. After a while, she straightened up, dropped her arms to her sides, and said, "Ann Marie, honey, Daddy needs to rest. You be quiet now, all right?"

She hustled past me and down the stairs. I followed her to their bedroom, stopping beside the bed while my mother flung open the medicine cabinet in their bathroom. One bottle at a time, she twisted off the cap and dumped its contents into her palm, separating and counting pills. After every bottle was lined in a row in front of the sink, I watched her mouth move and her head shake back and forth as she muttered, "He took all of today's pills. There's none missing. He took every pill he was supposed to. Why is he seeing things again?"

She gripped the edges of the vanity, tipped her face toward the ceiling, and yelled, "Goddamn you, why is he seeing things again?" She waited a beat and when nobody answered her, she slid to her knees and then onto her side until her cheek rested against the tile floor. She closed her eyes and said, "Why can't it *ever* be over? Lord, don't you see I'm so tired?"

I wanted to help her in some way, but at that young age, I didn't know what to do. As she was begging God to show mercy on her, I tiptoed backward across the carpet and out their bedroom door, shutting it softly behind me.

October 1968

THE LEAVES HAD already begun fading from green to orange, yellow, and red when Leo Dobbins showed up outside our front door. Dusk was darkening the sky as he stood underneath the unlit light on our porch, a few inches taller than me, maybe five foot six, with thick lips and a nose that spread wide across his face. He was slope-shouldered, thick-waisted, stubby-legged, and a few light strands of gray wove through his dark hair just above the ears. In his black hands, he carried a scuffed leather pouch. I swung back the door and my eyes widened. He was so black that, in the fading sun, he seemed to soften around the edges, and if it hadn't been for the camel-colored jacket, he probably could've blended right into the sky.

"I'm Leo. Your daddy in?"

I nodded but didn't budge from blocking the door. Jolene leaned against the doorjamb and said, "Why, you're colored!"

Leo smiled faintly, and I noticed the thin sheen of sweat that shined his forehead. I supposed he'd gotten many narrowed eyes uptown, men demanding why some negro had business out here, women pulling babies a little closer against their bodies, children whispering, gawking, laughing. He clutched the pouch tighter between his fingers and said in a soft voice, "That I am. Your daddy in?"

"I've never seen a colored man," Jolie said.

"Course you have," I said, "on TV."

"This is different. He's standing here on our stoop."

Leo said, "Last time I saw you was in a picture your daddy sent. You was just babies back then. You all got big."

"I got tall," Jolene said then pointed at me. "Marie just got fat."

Over the past summer, Jolene had spurted a head above me and was, like my father used to be, thin and sinewy. I was squat like my mother, thick around the waist, with breasts that had sprouted and gave my body curves, embarrassing me. The doorknob felt hot and clammy against my palm. I whispered, "I'm not fat."

"Course you ain't," Leo said. "Can't judge a girl till she done growing. You just ain't done yet."

"Mama said baby fat melts away," I said. "The older you get."

"Daddy!" Jolie yelled toward the kitchen. "Door's for you." To Leo, she said, "Marie's thirteen. That's no baby."

My father ambled to the door, his movements sluggish and his voice slow. For months, stronger dosages of the medicines had been building in his system, changing his appearance, his angular face now round and doughy, his once-lean body sporting a paunch that pushed out the waistband of his pants. He said, "Hello, Dobbins. Sorry the kids got no manners. Come on in."

Earlier in the year, after the only physician in town, Dr. Maisley, had increased his medications and my father started to wander the house late at night then sleep on the couch during the day, I asked my mother as she made breakfast, "If he's so sick, why can't he go to the hospital?"

"The hospital's not a nice place, Ann Marie."

"I was at the hospital when my leg broke. It's not that awful."

"Daddy would go to a different hospital. There'd be a lot of other people like him there."

"Why would that be bad?"

She faced me and said flatly, "They would stick wires onto your father, make him bite a piece of metal, and send electric shocks through his body. That's how they treat what he has."

She turned back to the stove, banging the skillet against the burner. I waited, seconds spilling into minutes, her words raising the hairs on my arms, before I asked quietly, "Why isn't the medicine working?"

She stopped folding the eggs and said, "It is working. Dr. Maisley said it'll be trial and error figuring out the right dosage." Softer, more to herself than me, she added, "It just *has* to work. There are no other options."

On the porch, Leo said, "Hello, Frank. Been a while."

My father's hand quaked as he thrust it out in greeting. Embarrassment flared red across his cheeks, and he dropped his arm back down to his side while his glance slid from Leo's dark eyes to his weathered brown boots. Staring at the plank-board floor, my father said, "Yeah. A long while. You brought it?"

Leo patted the scuffed pouch and said, "Yep. Just like you asked."

"Brought what?" Jolie asked.

"Nothing," my father answered, leading Leo across the threshold then through the living room and kitchen until they ended up in the foyer beside the stairs to the basement. "It's something between us men."

The basement door clattered shut, leaving Jolene and me staring at a black knothole in its wood.

"Who's that man?" she asked.

I shrugged.

After a few minutes, Jolie pressed her ear to the door and, after hearing nothing, whispered, "You want to know what they're talking about?"

"How?"

"There's a secret way in." She yanked me into the kitchen by one arm and pointed at the pantry door. "There's two boards missing in the floor near the back. You can see right down into the basement."

"Mama'll hear us."

"She's up in the attic humming and sewing. She won't hear a thing."

"Then they'll see us."

"Not if we're quiet."

"Daddy'd get mad if he found us there."

"So we got to be quiet, is all."

"What if he finds us?"

"He won't. You wanna go?"

Jolene picked her way through a corridor some four-feet long filled with cans of peas and carrots, mason jars of peaches and jellied grapes, burlap bags with potatoes and onions, and a round tin container full of flour. She motioned at me to come on, and I breathed deep, stepped inside, and shut the door behind me. We laid on our bellies in the darkness, legs bent at the knees, heels curling toward our behinds, eyes peering over the edge of the missing floorboards and into the basement, breathing as shallow as we could to keep the smell of onions and mouse droppings from swamping us.

"Can you see Daddy?" Jolie whispered.

"Yes."

The basement, except for the washing machine and clothes dryer propped up on shipping pallets, was empty because water trickled through the stone foundation like so many small streams when it rained. A few bare bulbs hung from the water pipes, shedding light in circles, and I could see my father and Leo Dobbins sitting below us with their backs to the stone wall and their legs sprawled in front of them. Between them sat a dented gray footlocker and a red plastic bucket that Leo thrummed his fingers against, rattling the ice and bottles of beer inside.

Leo grabbed a beer, uncapped it, and said, "Why you calling me, Frank?"

My father leaned over and took his own bottle. He brought it to his lips, tipped his head back, and stared at the ceiling while he drank deeply. Afterward, he smacked his lips and wiped his mouth with the back of his hand. "Something

ain't right with my head. Something ... I wanted to know ..."
He paused and took a few slow, deep breaths. He dropped his
arm, and the bottle clinked against the dirt floor.

"Know what, Frank?"

My father fiddled with the bottle's label, running the edge
of his fingernail along it, ripping at the paper. "If you've been
feeling okay? If there's been anything wrong with your head?"

"Like headaches?"

"No ..." My father huffed out a breath then bolted down
another slug of beer. "It's more like something that don't
square with the way you used to be before you went to Korea."

Leo leaned forward with his stretched face — wide eyes,
wide nose, wide lips. "Don't square?"

"I can't explain it better than that. Something just ain't
right."

"You still seeing things that ain't real?"

In the dark pantry, with heat pouring off my body as
I crowded beside Jolene, I sucked in my breath and nearly
gave us away. I understood quite clearly, as some dank, musty
smell filled my nose, that there'd be no more keeping secrets
because other people, people far away from Stanhope, Ohio,
knew about my father's illness, too.

"How'd you know that?" my father barked.

"Sarge said you was talking funny before he stuck you on
that chopper for Seoul. Said he handed you a cup of water
and you was acting like it was a live grenade."

"And then what?"

"Then nothing. You chucked the water and the bird
dusted off. I ain't heard from you except Christmas cards
since then."

Leo propped his beer between his thighs then unzipped the scuffed pouch he'd brought. He pulled out a plastic bag filled with crushed green leaves and a small stack of square white papers. He hiked it toward my father and said, "Smoke?"

Jolie's eyes narrowed and her mouth made a thin, tight line. Her fingernails curled and dug into the wood. She didn't utter one word, but I heard her loud and clear. Over the past summer, she and Patrick got caught with a marijuana joint underneath the front porch. My mother had come out to ask my father what he wanted for dinner, stopped with her wet hands curled in the folds of her apron, and sniffed the air. She bent over and peered between the boards, sweet smoke wafting up between the cracks, Jolene's blue eyes staring back. My mother hauled my sister onto the front lawn by the collar of her T-shirt, snatched the joint from between her fingers, threw it to the ground, and stamped on it with the heel of her house slipper. Patrick stood dumbly next to Jolie while my mother harangued her, with a finger alternating between Jolene and the joint, about the dangers of drugs. The words *crazy* and *fool* got used more than once. All the while, our father swayed on the porch swing, one foot kicking against the floorboards, while his head nodded along, *yes, yes, that's right.*

In the basement, my father rolled a fat cigarette, his thick, red tongue licking the edge of the paper to seal it. He toked up and blew a ball of smoke into the air. In a rough voice, he said, "I need to know about that day, Dobbins." Then he cracked open the footlocker and grabbed a handful of pictures, pitching them toward Leo so they fanned out across the floor. "These are the only memories I got."

My father's friend pinched a dog-eared picture the size of a baseball card in his stubby fingers. He exhaled so that smoke curled slow and lazy around his head then whistled low under his breath. "What you need to know?"

My father leaned forward, his voice dropping a notch lower. "Things were right with me before the hill?"

"Things was right with everybody before that damn hill."

"But me, Leo?" My father drank some more beer then belched softly. "Things were all right with me?"

Leo's joint smoldered between his fingers. He shook the beer bottle, flicking beads of water across the floor. "You didn't act no different than usual. That what you want to know?"

"But after? After I got shot?"

"You didn't know where you was. Sarge said you was talking funny before the chopper took you. Wasn't nobody else saw you after that. Hospital and then home. Man, that's all I know."

My father stubbed out his joint on the stone wall where it left a black smudge on a gray rock. "Me and you got to be friends over there, right?"

Leo sucked on the lip of the bottle then said, "Yeah."

"You'd tell me what was real, right?"

"Yeah."

My father's voice dropped again. "Something ain't right in my head. I see things that don't belong here in Ohio. Not in this town or on this farm ... or in this year."

Leo wiped his chin with his sleeve. "You talking about things from the war?"

The sump pump kicked on, and my father startled. His eyes shot around the basement, from the insulation spilling in yellow tufts between the water pipes to the one small window near the clothes dryer, black plastic ducting like a smooth snake curving underneath the window's metal frame. "One minute, a thing'll be a fishing lure in my fingers; the next, it'll be one of them Asian beetles." My father's hands started to shake, and he watched them quake, muttering, " 'It's survival of the fittest,' the sarge said. 'You ain't fit, you don't survive.' "

"What, Frank?"

"You ain't fit, your hands don't work, your mind don't work, you don't survive."

"There's no war on now," Leo said.

"Vietnam," my father answered.

"That ain't our war."

After a time, my father said, "The worst is up at the Sparkle Market in town; there's little girls playing around the poles underneath the awning." He stared at the floor, his voice dipping down to near a whisper. "But in my head, they're those little whores who used to sling their hooches for a few bucks. I got to work real hard to tell myself they're just some little kids."

"Bastard," Jolie hissed, her body stiffening against mine.

My father grabbed another beer, and water dripped from its glass bottom. Scared, I started to count the droplets that stained the floor, then my father's trousers, and finally his shirt as he began to drink.

"You ain't told nobody else?" Leo said.

Six drops of ice water darkened the cotton weave of my father's pants when he smacked the bottle against his thigh. "Not the whole truth. My wife ... I'm afraid she'd leave me if she knew how bad it was."

"Your kids?"

"They don't know neither."

"Bullshit," Jolie hissed, eyes on our father. "*Everybody* knows there's something not right with you. You ain't hiding a thing."

"You been to a doc?" Leo said.

"I been there. I got medicine. But even he don't know how bad it is. War's still chugging along in my gut. I see that little boy buried to his knees in the muck of the rice paddies. I see him clear as day staring up at the sky and screaming."

"Frank, you got to—"

"What's worse is that sometimes ..." My father paused, rested his beer on the floor near his hip, then tugged a thick black wallet from his front pocket. He rifled through a few dollar bills and pulled out a creased photograph with blue ink smeared across its back. He showed it to Leo and said, "Sometimes I'm only about fifty percent sure my kids are my kids. I got to keep pictures of them in my wallet to remind myself who they are. I got their names written on the back in case I forget."

A point in the center of my forehead began to ache. I thought about all the times my father had sat next to me, his wallet open in his lap, leafing through pictures of Jolie and my mother and me sheathed in plastic. He would slip them out, flip them over, and smile as he ran a fingernail across the names and dates written in a loopy scrawl on the back. It had never occurred to me that my father wasn't recalling something cherished but was instead coaching himself to remember who we were. Right then, I hated Leo Dobbins for the sweetness of his cologne and the sourness of his breath, for the way he made my father squat among his memories. That feeling made my mouth go dry. It made my stomach lurch and bitterness fill my mouth.

"Frank, you got to let that go."

My father dropped the photograph of Jolene and me onto the floor between his legs then leaned over and snatched the picture Leo was holding out of his fingers. He hollered, "We killed all them people! We killed them, and we didn't even know them well enough to hate them!"

"Better for us, man," Leo said softly, his nostrils flaring, "if they all got dead. Ain't no other way to be sure they wasn't gonna shoot us later."

My father grimaced, cupping the old photograph against his palm, curling his fingers into a fist, crumpling the paper so creases cut through his young uniformed body. "You sound like the sarge."

"I'm just a soldier who got sense. You forget the way it was, Frank. Wasn't just the soldiers carrying ammo. No, man, you got the kids and their mamas. You got the old ladies."

My father echoed, "The old ladies."

"You got that right. The old ladies. Don't tell me you be feeling sorry for the old ladies." Leo jerked his beer bottle toward my father, and water droplets flew everywhere, hitting Leo and my father and the floor with hushed plops, so the numbers I held in my head, the order and rhythm that comforted me, got jumbled and lost. "Ain't us ought to be sorry. That old biddy was carrying ammo. If she wouldn't a been humping for the gooks, she wouldn't a died like that."

"But she blew up. She just ... exploded."

Leo's thick, black thumb smoothed a white square of paper on his thigh. He tapped out a small mound of marijuana, smoothed it flat, and rolled another joint. "Hell, wasn't anybody *aiming* at her, Frank. A round hit some powder and, man, that old biddy lit up."

"I never seen anything like that," my father whispered. "Bones and blood and skin covering the ground. Her fingers lying near my boots."

"Don't tell me you felt bad."

"No." My father let the balled photograph roll from his unclenched fist onto the floor next to the smiling faces of Jolene and me. "Christ, I didn't feel bad at all. That's what's wrong with it. I didn't feel bad at all."

Leo toked up then passed the cigarette to my father. "Shooting gooks ain't like shooting birds."

My father pulled the sweet smoke into his lungs, blew it out, and said, "I shot a barn swallow with a BB gun once. I felt so bad about killing it, I never shot a gun again."

"Till Korea."

"Yeah, till Korea."

"You know the difference?"

My father sucked on the joint again, closing his eyes and saying, "Huh-huh."

"You ain't got to go up to the gooks and eyeball them after they dead. You just got to kill them and move on. Just like when the war's over, man. You just got to say it's a done thing and move on. Ain't no reason to pick it up and look at it. Ain't no reason to understand it."

"All those people who won't know their kids."

Leo drained his beer. "It's over, man."

My father roared up, pointing at the photographs scattered on the floor between them. "It ain't over for me. Don't you get it? I still see them. I can't sleep at night. The dark makes me afraid."

Leo's eyes scanned my father's face. In a low tone, he said, "Frank, it's over. I don't mean no disrespect. But it's over. You got to see that."

"My wife says I sleep with my eyes open. That once she touched me because she thought I was awake, and I damn near took her arm off."

I remembered my mother speaking to Jolene and me not long after that happened, telling us not to bother our father unless he was walking around and talking. When I asked why, she said, "So he can see you. That way you'll be safe."

Leo said, "I'm sorry, man."

Smoke hung in the air like a fog as my father said, "This ain't about you, Dobbins. It's about a mistake. Something I did a long time ago, and now there's no fixing it. Army said I could have money for college. All I wanted was to get some schooling so me and Adele could get out of this town."

Leo drew his legs toward his chest and rested his forearms atop his knees. "Nobody wanted nothing different. You think I wanted to see some kid's cheek all ripped up and pus leaking out his neck?"

"I still see him, that boy. I see his face and them black eyes staring me down."

"What's the use, Frank? It don't change nothing about what happened."

Lines cut across my father's forehead. He stared with a soft focus at the gray, brown, and black stones behind Leo's head. "I still hear him screaming up at the sky."

"Screaming at God."

My father said flatly, "Ain't no God."

"What you mean, 'no God'? That was the only reason for that war. Killing gooks 'cause they all Godless. 'Cause they don't know nothing about being good Christians."

My father stubbed out the joint on the floor. When he finally answered, he seemed tired, beaten. "There just ain't no God that would've let Korea happen. You seen the television? You seen that colonel in Vietnam blow the brains out of that guy in the middle of the street? There's no God would've let *that* happen."

"What? That don't even make sense. Them gooks was spreading Communism, man. *Communism.* Next thing, we don't stop them, and they be in our backyards, killing our own women and kids."

Suddenly, my father clapped his palms to his ears. "All that blood. All them screaming, '*Manzai. Manzai. Manzai.*' I can still hear it. Sometimes I think I'll go out of my head with that noise ringing in my ears."

"Aw, Christ, man." Leo sifted around in the photographs, found what he was looking for, and lifted it toward my father. "You remember our company? They all here in this picture. You know what we got to be proud of? We done most of them missions by ourselves, Frank. Got *that* to be proud of. The help they said was coming never came. Look at it, Frank. That was all of us. Ones who made it, and ones who didn't.

You made it. You got *that* to be thankful for. War's over, and you made it."

"Whole time I was there," my father said, his voice slow and thick, "I was looking over my shoulder down some empty, red dirt road. I was always waiting for help to come. Waiting for God to show up. Nobody ever came. Sometimes my life still feels like that."

Leo reached over and patted my father's leg. "You ain't by yourself now. Why'd you call me here? What you need?"

My father leveled his eyes at Leo and said, "What happened to my hip? You were there, right? What happened to get me sent home?"

Leo's head rocked backward in surprise. "You don't know?"

"I don't remember. I never remembered." My father skimmed his hand across his right hip. "All they said was I got the million-dollar wound, the one that'd get me sent home."

"It's been nearly seventeen years." Leo paused, searching my father's face for the punch line of the joke. Finding none, he blurted, "You ain't known for seventeen years?"

My father said, "No."

"The sarge didn't write you? Nobody said nothing?"

"I got a couple medals. Army gave me a Purple Heart 'cause of my hip. Got me a hunk of bronze, too, that they said was for bravery in action. Never said why."

Beside me, Jolene wiggled back and forth, fingers curled around the floorboards, inching herself closer to the edge.

Leo said, "Ambush, man. Right in the middle of some field at the base of that hill. Gooks firing machine guns, and us with no cover. Malone got gutshot. He was on the ground by your feet with his insides spilling out. You remember that?"

My father shook his head.

"You was hauling up that hill with a grenade in your hand. Headed right for them, and the grenade ended up being a dud. Damn thing don't go off, and there you was going down in the dirt with bullet holes all over the side of you. Shot you up good, they did. Doc said you must've been in shock. You had a gun right next to you, but you didn't move. We was all diving to the ground, and you was just lying there, staring up at the sky like all was right with the world."

My father's stiff face softened. He mumbled, "They were coming for me."

Leo leaned inward. "You remember now?"

In a faraway voice, my father answered, "Sometimes I dream of faces coming at me, walking slow, taking their time 'cause they see I can't move. They're smiling at me. My leg feels like it's on fire, burning up the side. Blood's pumping out a hole in me, and chips of my bone are on the ground. They got guns, and they point them at my head. I see their slanty eyes, and even their eyes are smiling at me. Then there's one hell of an explosion, and I wake up."

Leo nodded along, lips spreading in a grin. "Explosion, my friend, be the United States Army at its finest. That help you was waiting for? It finally came. Except it took out half the damn field we was crouching in. When the dust settled, those two gooks was history. There was nothing but a big damn hole. You was at the lip of it, babbling about something didn't make sense to nobody."

"What was I saying?"

"Nobody knew. Just babbling. Christ, I don't even remember. It's been a long time."

"What was I doing?"

"Just lying there. Blood pumping out of your hip. Pieces of bone on the ground. Just like that dream of yours."

My father waited, his eyes on Leo's mouth, but when no more words came, he asked, "That it?"

Leo glanced at the photographs spread on the floor, young faces staring up at him. "Lot of the unit got killed. Malone went down. Bigs Perry died. Dereks and O'Connor bit it. Sarge took a round in the shoulder."

"You?"

"Me? Hah! I lived to fight another day. Gave me a week off, time enough to get stinking drunk, then shipped me to another unit." He grabbed another beer from the bucket, thumbed the cap, and said in a quiet voice, "Hell, what're we talking about this for?"

My father sucked in a deep breath, blew it out, and said, "You see any of the other guys?"

Leo swilled beer around in his mouth then swallowed. "Sometimes the sarge be over at the VA Hospital in Wilkes-Barre. Plays a mean game of checkers, that one." He set his beer down and fished through the plastic bag of marijuana, pulling out a white square to ready another joint. "Mostly, Frank, ain't no guys want to remember."

"Wilkes-Barre?"

"Pennsylvania. Be a few hours from where I live."

"That ain't too awful far from here. You think that hospital could help me? You think they could do something without putting me on a psychiatric ward? Without locking me up?"

Leo sighed heavy, and if his breath would've had weight, it would've clunked to the ground. "I'll get you the number, and you call. Doctors can maybe do something for you. Better than doing nothing."

But something in Leo's sigh had given a loud and brutal answer to my father's questions. His lips pulled into a frown, and he eked out, "Okay."

Leo struck a match, and the thick scent of sulfur filled the air. He lit the joint then watched the match as it burned toward his fingers. He blew out the flame and said, "Frank?"

"Yeah?"

"Say something to your wife, man. She can help you."

"Yeah," my father said. He stood up, carried the bucket to the sink beside the washing machine, and dumped the icy water down the drain. He watched it swoop and circle, much like his life, disappearing like that into the dark, just a few shards, a few memories too big to fit, but soon those would melt, too, and then there'd be nothing of the person he was before the war; there'd be only this crazy person in his place.

My father lumbered back to where Leo sat against the wall with his face in the shadows, eyes closed, smoke swirling around his head, and scooped a half-dozen empty beer bottles into the bucket.

"You want me to leave the weed?" Leo asked.

"Naw, you take it. I ain't supposed to smoke it, just like I ain't supposed to drink."

My father sat beside him, and they talked in low tones about Vietnam, President Johnson, and all the boys who were dying. I nudged an elbow into Jolene's side and whispered, "C'mon, let's go. They're done." I inched backward until my feet smacked wood then reached up and cracked the door open so a blade of light poured inside. Jolene hadn't budged.

"C'mon," I whispered.

Jolene put a finger to her lips. "Shhh."

"C'mon," I said again.

My sister crept up to me and, with her face inches from mine, said, "I want to stay."

"Why?"

Her breath was warm and sweet on my face. "His hopes are gone. I want to see him the way he wants to see me."

Shocked, I said, "What?"

"He grinds me down. He wants there to be nothing left."

"What're you talking about?"

"Marie, there's a lot you don't see. There's lots of things you don't know at all."

She turned and crawled away. I watched her slip quietly into the darkness while I clutched at my chest, her words crushing against me there.

I squeezed past the pantry door as my father heaped the scattered photographs back into his dented gray footlocker, snapped the lid shut, locked it, and pocketed the key. Minutes later, Leo and my father stood awkwardly in the foyer.

"You call, you need anything," Leo said, stuffing his hands in his jacket pockets. "Pennsylvania be right next door, and my house ain't but an hour's drive away."

"All right," my father answered, the footlocker on one hip and the red plastic bucket on the other.

"Goodbye." Leo nodded at me as I stood in the kitchen, shifting my weight from foot to foot. "Maybe I see you again."

"Bye," I said.

My father turned at the sound of my voice. "Where's Jolene?"

I shrugged.

My father nodded toward the door. "Goodbye, Dobbins."

"See you 'round, Frank."

Less than two hours after he first showed up, my mother having never come down to meet him, Leo sunk into the driver's side of a rusted gray Chevelle and drove away, red taillights fading into nothing as he rounded the first curve in the road. My father barged outside, dropping the bucket and its empty bottles into the garbage can beside the house. With the footlocker clasped against his chest like some sort of shield, he plodded toward the barn. Standing in the foyer, my blue jeans and wool sweater dusty from the pantry, my white socks dark with grime, I watched him go, anger festering in my low belly for the things I didn't know and for the suffering thrust upon Jolene and me that had nothing, really, to do with us at all.

January 1969

IT WAS A Sunday morning when Jolene and I bustled around the living room, packing three worn cardboard boxes marked *X-mas Stuff* with two wreaths, several yards of silver tinsel, an armful of ornaments, and a nativity missing the baby Jesus. We hauled the boxes up to the attic, the wood stairs creaking under our weight, and pushed them across the floorboards until they came to a stop near an old bicycle with a dented wheel rim.

I pulled my robe tighter around my waist as I stood in the center of a thousand things no longer of use to anybody: a busted birdcage, a model train gray with dust, a velvet music box whose ballerina no longer danced, the husk of a sunflower tipped to one side and spilling hollow wilted seeds, a purple feather boa faded from the sun, a tricycle with one wrinkled pink ribbon still hanging from the handlebar, a huge cardboard box filled with hundreds of paperback books. My mother's hobby cluttered one corner: a manual sewing machine, a charcoal-colored dress mannequin, a woven basket chock full of threads and yarns.

Jolie turned on her heel, her long hair in a ponytail down her back, and spied, underneath a sawhorse soft with rot and somewhat hidden by a dark green tarp, the edge of our father's dented gray footlocker. She shuffled toward it, squatted down, and sat on her heels beside it while the single bare bulb above her head threw light in a bright circle.

"You want to look at that medal he got from the army?"

A spec of a doubt gnawed at me so I said, "Huh-huh."

Jolie fingered the footlocker's silver lock. "What about a picture of our dead baby brother?"

It had been so long since she'd mentioned the baby that, years ago, I decided she'd made it all up. Thinking she was lying, I said, "All right."

She blew the bangs out of her eyes and said, "It's locked. You got something with a flat edge?"

I glanced around. "Maybe somewhere in all this stuff."

"Find something flat. Something I can jam under the lock to pop it."

"You won't break it, right?"

"Naw, I won't break it."

"Because then Daddy'd know we were up here snooping."

I found a pair of scissors in my mother's sewing basket, and Jolene hooked one blade in the keyhole, wheedling it back and forth. Something cracked then the latch flung open.

"You broke it," I said, crouched beside her.

Jolene dropped the scissors near her hip and tossed back the footlocker's lid. "Might've."

"Daddy'll be mad."

"It's too late now, Marie. C'mon." She sifted through dog-eared pictures, yellowed letters, and a dried red rose petal pressed flat between wax paper. She handed each thing to me, and I spread them on the floor next to us.

She passed me a scratched copper-colored key with a red loop of yarn through its hole. The loop was a necklace so I tugged it over my head, and the key fell between the folds of my robe, dangling between my breasts. Heat rushed to my face, blood pooling in my cheeks. I was three months shy of fourteen years old and hated the feeling of those mounds pushing out my shirts. I whipped the necklace off and dropped it on the floor. I watched my sister in her nightgown — tall, thin-hipped, flat-chested — dig through the footlocker and ached to be her. She was focused on finding that picture, tossing items toward me without thinking, one of which was a faded newspaper clipping, dated 1952, with a thumbnail picture of my father in a dark army uniform.

LOCAL BOY AWARDED
THE BRONZE STAR & PURPLE HEART
STANHOPE, OHIO —
In a simple ceremony at the town's square, Lt. Gen. John Bradley, First U.S. Army Commander, pinned the Bronze Star and the Purple

Heart on Frank Adler, a Korean War veteran. During the ceremony, Bradley commended Adler for his "extraordinary heroism in the face of extreme danger."

Adler joined the Army in 1949, and when the war on the Korean peninsula erupted, he was on his way to the Infantry Division in Korea. The eastern front was brutal and harsh, riddled with shelling and rifle fire. When winter arrived, Adler's squad of nine was ill-equipped for the horrendous cold. Moving northward, they fought each day in the subzero temperatures with only field jackets to keep them warm. At night, they chipped foxholes into the frozen earth. The territory was dangerous, and no fires were allowed for cooking. Often, Adler and his fellow soldiers ate frozen C-rations. Sleep was often fleeting.

Bradley went on to say, "Private Adler arrived home in America to a population who called this war unjust, called it a police action. But Frank Adler knew different. He'd been on the front lines. He'd seen the horrible faces of war, the brutality that one person can do to another, even to women and children, even to the elderly."

Adler was wounded in action and discharged from the Army. He continues to live in Stanhope and will soon be marrying his fiancée, Adele Morton.

I rubbed the newsprint between my fingers, but the ink had long since dried. My father looked young and sad. His light-colored eyes stared back at me. His mouth was a rigid line with just the very tips slanting downward. I touched his face, and the dry paper made a tiny *scritching* sound. I started to mouth the words, *This Little Light of Mine*, but Jolie tossed another object at me, and my hands loosened in surprise. The article fell to the floor and in my lap sat the small carving of the baby Jesus that belonged in our Christmas nativity scene. His wooden face, smattered with tiny gashes, had been chipped off.

"You seen this?" I said.

Jolie glanced over her shoulder. "Yeah. What happened to it?"

I ran my fingernail across its face. "Don't know."

"Those look like knife marks," she said. "Like it got stabbed."

"Its face is gone," I said. "I wonder why Daddy did that?"

"He's crazy, that's why." She turned back to the footlocker, rifled through it, then thrust a photograph into the space between us. "Hah! I told you we had a brother."

It was a round-faced baby, his skin wrinkled, one eyelid shut, the other slightly raised. His eyelashes were long and dark, eyebrows thin, nose a bit small for his face. His scalp was covered with a few dark curly hairs whisked up in a cowlick near his forehead. One pale hand was curled into a tight fist near his cheekbone.

"He's even got the stork bite like we had," Jolene said.

"Huh?"

"The mark on his forehead. Same as both of us when we were born."

"He's so little."

"He's dead," Jolie said flatly.

Staring into my lap, I fiddled with the baby Jesus while a twinge of sadness crimped my gut. Suddenly, Jolie made a whining sound, and when I looked up at her, she'd gone the color of ashes. The skin beneath her right eye began to twitch. Behind me, our father stood with one booted foot on the top step, the other on the floorboards, only a yard or so from where my sister and I huddled beside his footlocker. His eyes bored first into me then into Jolene.

His voice went low and deep, growling, "What're you doing?"

Jolie whipped her hands in front of her to push herself up but knocked into me and sent the baby Jesus sailing toward the box marked *X-mas Stuff*. Her heel caught the scissors used to jimmy the lock, and they went skittering across the floor in our father's direction. She shot upward, backing away from our father, eyes darting, trying to figure out how to escape.

"We were just looking," I stammered.

My father glared at us, his brow furrowed, his eyes narrowed. Droplets of sweat beaded near his hairline. His fingers curled into fists, released, then curled again. "I knew you two would be up here. I seen you sneaking around camp. I seen you waiting for a time I wasn't looking so you could steal my stuff."

I whispered, "We were just looking."

My father stomped toward me, roaring, "What'd you take?"

Eyes on my father and not where she was going, Jolie backpedaled, tripping over the edge of a box and falling onto a plastic garbage bag, her weight blowing out the bottom corner so dull-colored puzzle pieces spilled in a small pile. She tumbled sideways, arms flailing to catch herself, and bruised easily as her behind smacked against the floorboards.

My entire body shuddered. My mouth dried and my stomach cramped. I said, "We didn't steal anything."

His face flared red, a vein near his temple began to throb, and from some deep, soured place within him, he exhaled with a smattering of spit and sound. "That's *my* stuff."

He closed the couple of feet between us and him in one long stride. He hurtled past me, eyes on Jolene, fingers like talons curling out in front of him, and grabbed her by the nape. My father hissed, "I've been waiting for you to try something. I seen you two sneaking around. 'They're up to something,' I told myself. Damn, if I wasn't right."

Behind him, I said again, "We didn't steal anything."

My father kept his eyes locked on Jolene. "If you weren't stealing, then what're you doing busting open my footlocker?"

"We'll buy you a new one," I whined. "We'll fix it."

He huffed a breath across my sister's small face. "That ain't the point. Point is you don't go stealing in the first place."

His grip tightened, and he jerked Jolie back and forth. A long time ago, in the dark, damp cellar, Jolie had vowed never to cry out again. But my father twisted the tiny, blonde hairs on the back of her neck until her eyes watered and she yelped in pain.

"You gonna cry now, *mama-san*? You gonna complain to the sarge?"

Jolene's fists punched at my father, striking his arms and landing one blow to his left cheekbone. His body rocked backward, his grip lessened, and Jolene kicked out, her sock-covered toes jamming against his shin. She curled forward, trying to get away, but my father's hand arced into the air, muscles rolling under his skin as the flat of his palm slammed into her head.

"Don't you *ever* fight me!" my father howled at her. "The good guys always win!"

My sister went limp against his grip. I watched with a tightness in my stomach that threatened to make me vomit as my father grinned and laid Jolene on the floor. His boot caught on the trash bag, stretching the black plastic before he jerked his leg twice, mashing in the side of the bag and kicking it away. He flattened his palm to Jolene's shoulder, his knee to her thigh, and pinned her to the floor. Beneath him, Jolie lay still, her face turned to the side, cheek to the floor, eyes in a dull focus, staring past the pink ballerina in the busted music box, while her mind slipped slowly away from her body.

My father leaned his face toward hers, and hot, angry words fell from his mouth. "How much you charge, *mama-san?*"

"Daddy?" I said softly behind him.

He paused, my voice buzzing like a cloud of black gnats in his head, and without turning, said, "Who?"

There was no telling what to say and what not to say to my father. I lived with fear low in my belly, pulsing in a knot above my pubic bone, that no matter what I did I would make it worse. But Jolie's glassy stare, the tremor in her legs beneath her nightgown, the bit of saliva that oozed along her chin, those things spurred me to eke out, "Daddy, leave her alone."

His broad back to me, his face inches from Jolene's, he said, "I ain't anybody's daddy. I ain't got any kids."

Right then, I remembered my mother years ago kneeling beside me in the bathroom, her hand cupping my chin so I would look her in the eye. "You listen to me," she'd said. "He ever does that again, you keep telling him over and over again who you are. Say, 'Daddy, I'm Ann Marie.' You understand?"

I whined, "Daddy, I'm Ann Marie." I thrust a shaking finger in my sister's direction. "And Jolene. That's Jolene."

My sister lay with her head turned, eyelids blinking every so often. Her legs spasmed, and the skin just below her right eye twitched. My father asked her, "A buck, two bucks? How much?"

"That's Jolene," I barked. "Jolene. Jolene. Jolene."

"Christ, how much?" My father jammed his fingers into the front pocket of his jeans and wrenched out a handful of crumpled dollar bills. "That's about four bucks. That enough?"

Jolie was nearly still. Her chest rose and fell. Her golden hair, loose from its rubber band, fanned out across the floor.

"Or maybe it should be free for you trying to steal my stuff."

I whispered, "Daddy, we weren't stealing anything."

My father whipped his head around, his eyes savage, his teeth bared. Sweat bloomed across his forehead and stained round patches along the collar of his red flannel shirt. The stink of manure rolled off his boots. "I ain't your daddy. I ain't *nobody's* daddy, you got that? You better shut up or you're next."

I wailed, "Look at her!" Then more quietly, "Please. It's Jolene."

My father narrowed his eyes and sniffed the air. "How come you smell like sweet alfalfa hay?"

Surprised, I stuttered, "I-I-I was in the barn this morning."

He cocked his head a notch. "Barn? What barn?"

"The one outside."

He muttered, "Reminds me of home." Then he faced Jolene again and ran a hand through the short hairs on his scalp. He fumbled with the buttons down the front of his shirt and stripped it from his torso, wadding it in a ball and tossing it to the side. Chicken pox had left small ovals on his back, and near his right hip, a thick, ragged scar rose from his waistband. My father cupped Jolie's thigh with his palm and pushed it outward.

On my behind, scooting backward toward the stairs, I yelled, "I'm going to get Mama!"

He craned his neck toward me and said, "Who?"

"Mama." A thought crashed through my head — *he didn't know her as a mother* — and I said, "Adele."

I watched his face soften. The creases in his forehead, the hard line of his jaw, the tight band of his lips, all the things that made him look enraged and unfamiliar, slackened. Meekly, he said, "Adele?" He faced Jolene and traced the edge of her body, slipping his fingertip from her cheek, along her shoulder, past her ribs, and lingering near her hipbones. "I got a girl back home named Adele."

"I'm going to get her."

"She ain't here. Sometimes I wish she was ..." His finger slid to Jolie's knee, where he touched the end of her nightgown and began to raise it upward. "Then again, I wouldn't wish this place on nobody."

My eyes darted around, searching for a weapon with which to bash him over the head and save Jolene. But somewhere in the close, dim quarters of my mind, a quiet voice rose up and said, *If your mother doesn't see what he's doing with her own eyes, this won't ever end.*

I swung my legs through the rectangular hole in the floor then yelled at my father's back, "I'm going to get her."

He straddled Jolie's thighs, his face dipping toward her chest. I could see the white of her underwear as my father breathed in deeply and closed his eyes, asking, "My girl?"

"She's just downstairs."

"She ain't here." My father's voice got gravelly and thick. "Ain't no real women here."

The house was steeped in an awful quiet. Jolie stared blankly at nothing at all. Time inched by, a minute, two, and still my father squeezed his eyes shut, breathing in the smell of my sister.

I barked, "I'm going to get her. She'll see what you're doing."

"She ain't here." He opened his eyes and touched the elastic of Jolene's underwear, slipping his finger beneath it. "You ain't just a thief but a liar, too."

I raced down the attic stairs, my robe billowing out behind me as I shouted for my mother. I rushed along the second-floor hallway then down the stairs and through the living room. Chest burning, legs rubbery, I shot into my parents' bedroom. My mother stood by the bed, pulling clothes from a basket on the floor, folding them against her body, and stacking them on the bed. The radio blared a country tune, and she hummed softly along.

The doorknob banged so hard against the wall that it left a mark, and my mother whirled around, her fingers opening and one of Jolie's yellow blouses falling to the floor. She blurted, "For goodness sakes!"

"Mama!" I screamed then spit out disconnected words, the thoughts running fast in my head, but my mouth working at half-speed. "Daddy. Jolene. Attic." And finally, the last word that felt sour and thick as paste in my mouth, "Rape."

My mother's face blanched. She dashed toward the door, stumbling over the laundry basket, going down on one knee. A low guttural noise came out of her throat. She scrambled up and tore past me, leaving me alone with the smell of lotion trailing behind her. I ran after her, climbing the stairs two at a time until we stood in the attic, gasping for breath.

The groin of my father's jeans pressed against Jolie's thighs. He had scooped her wrists together in his left hand and pinned them above her head. Grease from his fingernails smudged dark marks against the light freckles of her forearms. His right fist hovered in the air, ready to strike. I could tell by the way her left cheek swelled, the skin above the bone just beginning to purple, that he'd already punched her at least once.

"Frank!" my mother screamed.

My father stiffened. Still hunched over Jolene, he glanced back at us, saying, "Christ, why's it got to be like this? Why they always got to go after *my* stuff?"

I tugged at the hem of my mother's sweater. "Mama, do something."

"Frank," she said softer. "It's Adele."

"Adele?" My father's fist eased down until it rested against his thigh. He dropped Jolie's wrists, and her arms fell limply against the floor. He straightened up and said, "I got a girl back home named Adele."

"I know, Frank." My mother moved toward him, stepping slowly, hands outstretched. "Honey, it's me. It's your girl, Adele. You need to stop what you're doing, Frank."

"You're not real," my father whispered. "My girl's far away."

"Yes, I'm real, Frank. Honey, you have to stop."

"But they were stealing." He motioned at the footlocker, at the pictures and mementos strewn around it, at the scissors used to bust the lock. "*Stealing.*"

"It doesn't matter, Frank. You have to stop."

Behind my mother, I whispered, "We weren't stealing."

"They got to learn," my father said flatly, his lips pulled back from his teeth. He swung around, fist arcing through the air and slamming into Jolene's cheek.

My mother yelled, "No, Frank!" Then softer, "Please, no."

Jolie's eyelids fluttered open, and she locked eyes with our mother. She waited a few seconds but when no other help was forthcoming, Jolie opened her mouth and screamed so hard that, within a minute, her voice went hoarse, finally petering out into nothing.

My father blinked. He stared blankly into Jolie's face. In Jolie's scream, in that high pitch of her young voice, was a sound all too familiar — one he knew well from nights dreaming with his eyes open: the screeching of a little village boy toward the sky as my father marched past with his squad, soldiers legs pumping past mothers and brothers and sisters face down in the muck; my father's own shriek when the son he was supposed to have came into the world unmoving, not even a day old before he got swallowed by a small mound of dirt in the front yard. Beyond that strangled sound, my father finally saw Jolene. He caressed her hair. He traced the curve of her ear. Jolie's chest heaved. Saliva slid from the corner of her mouth. My father cupped her chin in his hand and tilted her face toward his.

"Jolene," he said, shaking his head. "It's Jolene."

My mother squatted down beside him and moved his hand away from Jolie's face. "Shhh. It's okay now. Everything will be just fine."

Rage pumped through my belly as I watched my mother console him, not punish him, while Jolie lay on the warped floorboards, twitching from time to time in the middle of all those crumpled dollar bills, her eyes in a thousand-yard stare, her face still as a plastic mask. But it was my father's hand that my mother was stroking.

He curled his forehead against my mother's breast, breath hitching as he cried, "It's Jolene. I didn't know it was Jolene."

"Shhh, Frank. It's okay. Calm down. We'll take care of this together. Just like always."

I moved over to my sister, sat cross-legged on the floor, and pulled her head into my lap. Her skin was cool and moist. Her hair stuck fast against her cheeks. She closed her eyes and whimpered softly against my legs.

My mother said, "Jolie, are you all right?"

My sister's tiny voice croaked, "There's a rabbit, it's going down a hole."

I ran my fingers gently across her forehead, gathering strands of sweat-slicked hair and tucking them behind her ear. I said, "What, Jolene?"

"It's getting buried. It's so dark in there."

"Jolie," I said softly, "there's no rabbit."

She squeezed her eyes tighter and held her breath. Later, she said, "Is he gone?"

I glanced at my father, sitting a few feet away, and said, "No."

My mother slung her arm around my father's waist, helping him to stand. To me, she said, "I'll take him downstairs, okay? It's all going to be fine. Ann Marie, you tend to your sister. I'll be right back."

I listened to their steps creaking the stairs then padding along the carpet. When I heard nothing, I curled my mouth to Jolie's ear and whispered, "He's gone. You can get up now."

She didn't move. In a faint voice, she said, "Head hurts. Face, too."

"He hit you. Do you remember?"

She nodded.

"He's gone now," I said. "We should go."

Jolie opened her eyes, the left one like a crimson stain from the force of my father's fist bursting blood vessels, and met mine. "You were right."

"About what?"

"Words don't work."

I didn't answer.

"Don't you remember?" Jolene asked, her voice thin. She paused. "Maybe not, it's been a long time."

"I remember," I said, grimacing for the hope I stole from her all those years ago in her bed, my mouth so close to her ear, her body trembling against mine.

"You were right."

"No, Jolie. I don't think so."

"Your words did nothing. Mama's words did nothing. But I screamed, and he stopped. You were right, Ann Marie. Words won't fix anything."

I remember feeling far away, the scope of my vision somewhat foggy, things seeming to shift and fade around me. I swayed back and forth, saying, "Maybe I'm dreaming."

Her words floating up from my lap, Jolie mumbled, "Mama won't help us. Words don't work. There's no dream. We're on our own."

I stroked the side of my sister's face and started to hum a slow tune. Jolene pressed against my hand, her left eye swelling shut.

Just behind me, near the box marked *X-mas Stuff*, the broken baby Jesus lay on its side. Inside the footlocker rested the dulled blade of the army knife that had whittled away its face. My father had clasped that figurine in his hand late one night, interrogating it in a hollow voice, "Why you doing this to me? Ain't I had it bad enough? Why you got to go and make me lose my mind, too? When you going to help me?" But when baby Jesus didn't answer, my father had taken the edge of the blade and sliced off its mouth, then its nose, and, finally, grasped the knife by the hilt and stabbed at Jesus's small face. That empty, vandalized face stared blankly in our direction.

It occurred to me, as the chill of the attic finally settled in, that I'd been humming *Amazing Grace*. I stared at Jolie's pummeled face then tipped my head to the ceiling, mouthing the words, "Jesus, will you save us now?" I waited, Jolie breathing softly in my lap, but there was no sound except the creak of the attic steps.

At the top of the stairs, my mother said, "Daddy's in bed. It's safe to come down."

At the sound of our mother's voice, Jolene rolled on her side, so her back faced our mother, and curled her knees toward her chest.

"I'm sorry," my mother mumbled. "You don't know how sorry I am."

"Why didn't you help us?" I said.

Her eyes darkened. "I wish I could take it back. I wish I would've known what to do."

"You could have stopped it." My voice rose in pitch with every word. "You could've done something, but you just stood there. *You just stood there.*"

"Ann Marie, I'm sorry. Jolie, honey ..." She paused, waiting for Jolene to acknowledge her. When my sister made no sound, our mother said, "I can't go back and change it now. All I can do is promise you it won't happen again."

She stepped toward us, and I threw a protective arm around Jolene.

"Please, Ann Marie," my mother pleaded.

"What about us?" I shouted. "When will *you* protect *us?*"

My mother sunk to the floor next to the stairs. "You don't make it easy, honey. I'm not saying what Daddy did was right. It wasn't right. But you girls don't obey when you're told. You girls go playing around with his things, and he gets mad. He's got a right to be mad. Those're his private things."

"Jolie didn't deserve that." I pointed at the bruise across her cheek.

"No, she didn't. Daddy was wrong. The punishment was too severe. But you have to understand, honey, that Daddy has a right to expect you to obey."

I looked everywhere but at my mother. Pictures were strewn about. The scissors lay askew on the floorboards. The footlocker's lid was flung open, its silver lock hanging cockeyed. Jolene closed her good eye and pushed her clasped fingers between her thighs.

After a while, my mother said, "There's something else we need to talk about."

I waited, watching the slow rise and fall of my sister's ribcage.

"Our dirty laundry," my mother started, "is nobody else's business. People here ... they like to talk. We need to, well, not tell anybody else about what happened. I don't want it to be hard for us to live in this town."

In that instant, I truly hated my mother. I despised her with a blackness that would steep in my belly for years afterward. My head felt as if it were spinning while I breathed in the smells of mothballs and old paper from the attic, peppermint from Jolene, strawberry lotion from my mother.

In a thin voice, my mother said, "We have to go downstairs now. We have to put some ice on Jolene's cheek."

I leveled my gaze at her. "You go and get the ice ready. We'll be down in a minute."

She frowned. It was a tiny gesture, but I knew what it meant. Even while she touted the value of my father's privacy, she didn't like the idea of secrets passing between Jolene and me. She didn't like it one bit.

After my mother descended the stairs, Jolie whispered, "How come she never helps us? How come she don't stand up for us the way she stands up for him?"

"She's weak-willed," I said.

Jolie opened her one good eye, rolled over, and stared at the place my mother had been. "No, Ann Marie, she's a disgrace.

February 1970

IT HAD BEEN over a year since my father stopped talking to Jolene and me. After the attack in the attic, when nobody knew what to say and so didn't say anything at all, his words became softer and fewer until finally he'd only speak to our mother, asking her to tell us this or that. He dawdled in the barn most days, no longer able to fix cars or work the fields, rather just filling time, avoiding us as best he could. Spring, summer, and fall hadn't been that bad; it was easy enough to find friends, hobbies, and long walks to occupy our time. But by the beginning of the year, when snow draped thick and heavy along the trees and the sky was always gray, the constant uncomfortableness of it — the heaviness in the air when my father came in a room, the prickling of my skin when he saw me, hesitated, then turned, head bowed, and scurried away — began to grate me down.

My mother had taken my father to Dr. Maisley every few months since the attack. Dosages were adjusted upward; new pills were tried. He took medications to control the schizophrenia, others to combat side effects, some to keep him awake, another to help him relax. My father remained at home, and my mother cared for him — making sure he bathed, shaving his face with a straight razor, counting out his pills and watching as he swallowed them, packing lunches he would take to the barn.

Jolie's bruises went from purple to blue then yellow and finally faded altogether. I learned to walk around without flinching at every small noise. I stopped glancing at my father's right temple, searching for the slight indent the gun barrel would leave after he pressed it there. Eventually, the overwhelming feeling of dread that used to swamp me when I woke every morning became nothing more than a slight twinge in my gut.

Creases grew around my mother's eyes and lips, gray threaded through her hair. Late at night, when she thought everyone was asleep, she would sit at the kitchen table with a mug of coffee cooling in front of her. She looked into the cup, her face reflected back, and started to cry. She'd shake her head, saying, "I can't put him in the hospital. I can't do that to him, not after everything he's been through already."

My father's face began to carry a stunned, leaden expression. He would stare at his limbs when he moved, as if they were somehow detached from his body. Once, he said out loud to no one in particular, "It's like I'm moving through thick sand. Sand up to my waist and me trying to walk through it."

Often at dinner, when Jolie and I sat quietly on either side of the table, faces near our plates and eyes shooting glances at each other, my father would complain to my mother, at first angrily then with a whine and finally begging, about the medications the doctor had prescribed.

"They're enormous!" he'd shout. "Horse pills."

"You have to take them," my mother replied calmly, slicing the chicken on her plate.

"I can't hardly swallow them."

"Break them in half."

"They taste bad that way."

My mother sighed and spoke firmly, a parent to a child. "Frank, you have to take them. There's no other choice."

He whined, "But it takes everything I got just to get out of bed in the morning."

My mother, as she always did, softened her tone. "It's better than the alternative. If you don't take those pills, you'll be sick again. Now eat before your dinner gets cold."

"It ain't fair. None of this was supposed to happen."

"Life isn't fair."

My father poked at the meat on his plate, the edge of it sliding into the mashed potatoes. "Please, Adele. I can't keep taking these pills. This ain't living."

Jolie would stare at her fork, pressing the tines into her peas, flattening them against the plate. Later, she'd tell me, "I liked him better before. At least he wasn't whining all the time. Least I didn't feel *ashamed* to know him."

My mother put a piece of chicken in her mouth, chewed and swallowed. "Disability won't pay unless you take your medicine. You can't work anymore. I can't work. Renting out the fields only pays so much. We need the money. You have to take the pills, Frank. There are no other options."

"I can't be a good father on the pills."

"You're a worse father off them."

With a frown on his face, he heaped the mashed potatoes, peas, and chicken into a mound on his plate. My mother would say, "Eat, Frank," and my father would pick at the pile, prying off a pea here, a ragged slice of chicken breast there. We ate like that nearly every night. After dessert, ice cream or maybe cake, my father would ask my mother to relay messages to Jolene or me.

"Can you tell Marie that stray dog she used to feed has been sniffing around again?" he said.

I glanced up at the sound of my name.

My mother motioned toward me and said, "You tell her yourself, Frank. She's sitting right there."

He studied his chocolate cake, the middle caved in where he'd dug at it with his spoon.

"It's okay, Daddy," I said.

My father stuffed a mouthful of cake onto his tongue, chewed and swallowed. With a few crumbs spraying as he spoke, he said, "I don't think anyone else feeds him."

My mother paused, her fork in midair. "Who?"

He dropped his spoon and curled his fingers around the edge of the table. "The dog. Marie needs to feed him."

"Frank, she's right here." My mother rested her fork against her plate. "Tell her yourself."

I stared at my father and waited. Jolene dipped her mouth closer to the table, her hair falling forward and hiding her face. My father squashed one crumb after another beneath his thumb then violently pushed his chair back from the table. "I just don't want him going hungry." Then he turned, shuffling off into the foyer and out the front door.

My mother shoved her plate away, cradled her forehead in her palm, and said, "When is this going to stop?"

I asked, "When's he gonna talk to us?"

Jolene, her head hovering inches from her plate and a small spasm jerking her chin, said, "Who cares?"

"Jolene!" my mother yelled.

"I mean it," Jolie answered quietly. "What difference does it make if he talks to us or not? He's crazy."

"He's not crazy," my mother said. She hesitated then added, "He's sick, Jolene. He has a disease."

Jolie snorted. "Sick? He seems to have been sick *forever*."

My mother dropped her hands into her lap and fiddled with the buttons of her blouse. More to herself than Jolene, she said, "The doctor told me not to tell you about your daddy's illness. He said you'd never understand. It's not about me or you or Ann Marie. Lord knows, I wish I could make it better, but I can't. I just can't. I don't know what else to do."

My father spent the next few days puttering in the barn and tinkering with the busted tractor. In the late afternoons, he walked the edge of the pine trees that lined the driveway, his boots caving holes in the snow. After school, I would lean against the living room window and watch him walk back and forth, noticing he was careful to plant his feet where he'd already stepped so there was only one set of prints.

My mother came up behind me, her breath fogging a spot on the pane.

"He's making sure he steps in the footprints he's already made," I said. "Why's he doing that?"

My mother brushed her fingertips against the glass. In a faint voice, she said, "That's what soldiers do when they're on watch."

"But who's Daddy watching for?"

"The enemy."

"But who's the enemy?"

"I don't know."

She hurried toward the kitchen and jerked the telephone from the cradle on the wall. She leaned her forehead against the cabinet that held the dinner plates. After a while, she said, "Yes, I'll hold," then started tapping her foot impatiently. Later, she said, "It's Adele Adler. Is Dr. Maisley available?" She waited a beat before adding, "It's urgent." Then, "Okay, well, can you ask him to call me? It's about Frank."

When I looked out the window again, my father was nowhere in sight. To this day, I don't know why I wandered into the foyer and slipped on my mother's black boots and my own navy peacoat. Snow churned against my face as I walked down the driveway, hands shoved deep in my pockets, head bent against the wind. At the edge of the tree line, I looked up at the slate-colored sky. It seemed so far away now.

I heard a branch snap and watched wet snow tumble to the ground. I breathed in the cold, sharp, tinny smell of winter. Soon, I caught a stench like something burning, that foul, smoldering odor that clung to my father, glistening in his pores from the medications. I turned, and he was a yard away from me. His hands and face were pale against the dark green of his jacket. Snowflakes dotted the scruff of his jawline.

Plumes of his breath fogged the air. He pointed at the ground and spoke directly to me for the first time in nearly a year. "I saw your prints."

Fear gnawed at my belly. I looked around, but we were alone. Finally, I said, "What'd you need, Daddy?"

A dark look crossed his face. He stared at me then at his palms. My mother, wearing only slacks, a sweater, and a pair of white socks, rushed through the front door and onto the wide whitewashed porch. Her shrill, scared voice sliced through the air. "Frank, what're you doing?"

My father trudged a few yards closer to the house and yelled into the wind, "Who's that girl by the pine trees?"

My mother cut her eyes to me. "You mean Ann Marie?"

"That's Marie?" he said softly. "She don't look like Marie."

My mother hurried down the porch stairs and across the snow-covered lawn with a finger pointing in my direction. She shouted, "That's Marie! Ann Marie! Your daughter!"

"Huh," my father said and turned to face me. His eyes had that same faraway look they'd had the day he slammed his fist into Jolie's soft face. "Sometimes, the edges of her blur."

Jolie appeared in her bedroom window, white curtains framing her face. My mother clasped an arm around my father's waist, shepherding him toward the house. I stood silently beside the creaking trees, cold air chafing my skin, and watched my parents disappear through the side door then watched Jolie's face vanish from the window. I wrapped my arms around my middle, feeling lost and alone, not knowing that within days I would be the catalyst for change in my family, that I would be the fuse to light a chain reaction.

THE FIRST EXPLOSION happened on Valentine's Day.

I was curled on the couch in the living room, my face buried in Steinbeck's *The Red Pony*, when my mother sashayed into the room with a ceramic bowl of tomatoes pressed against her stomach and said, "I need you to slice these up for the dinner salad."

Without looking up, I said flatly, "I'm busy."

I could feel her eyes boring into the top of my head. I stared at the pages of my book, words blending together. My face felt hot and prickly.

"Marie," she said, a fine edge to her voice, "first of all, you don't talk to me that way. And second of all ..." She leaned over with the bowl of tomatoes still pressed to her belly, grabbed my chin, and forced it upward, "you look at me when you speak to me."

She had no right to be angry, I decided. If anyone, *I* had the right to be furious for every time Jolene and I came second to our father's needs or the neighbors' opinions. I yelled, "Why?"

My mother simply said, "It's respectful."

The tangled knot in my belly, the one just above my pubic bone, gave a sharp twinge, and I said, "I don't respect you."

The air between us flattened. She released my chin. Her grip on the ceramic bowl loosened, and it tumbled to the floor. Small, ripe tomatoes rolled slowly across the carpet. Her voice dropped low and soft, without conviction. "Young lady, you respect your elders."

I snapped my book closed. "You don't just *get* respect, you *earn* it. You haven't earned mine. Not by a long shot."

She narrowed her eyes and blushed a bright crimson. "Don't you talk to me like that."

The knot inside me unraveled, braided cords loosening and ricocheting through my body. My heart thundered in my chest. My stomach felt queasy. "Go to hell!"

She lashed out and grabbed the front of my shirt, the top button popping off and sailing toward the ground. She hauled me upward off the couch until I stood nearly nose-to-nose with her. Her nostrils flared, blowing hot, dry breath across my face. I braced myself with one foot behind the other, knees slightly bent. "*I* never spoke to my mother that way!" my mother shouted. "*I* never disrespected her like that!"

My gut cramped. I didn't want to be anything like her — to have the same squat body, the same wide hips and brown eyes, the same one dimple on the left cheek when we smiled. Mostly, I didn't want to ever make the choices she did. I hollered, "I'm not you! Thank God, I'm not you!"

My mother did a thing she had never done before and would never do again after that day. Her arm shot out and her palm came sideways across my face, catching my cheekbone and then the edge of my reading glasses. The frames slammed hard against the bridge of my nose before falling off my face, one eyepiece popping out as they hit the ground.

The force of the blow sent me staggering backward, my heel landing on a tomato and its skin bursting beneath my weight. Red juice and green seeds squirted across the light-colored carpet. The backs of my knees smacked against the couch, and I sat down with a grunt. Something in the tomato's ripped skin, in its innards seeping into the floor, made the lines on my mother's face ease. "I'm sorry," she said. "I shouldn't have done that."

She stepped toward me, hands outstretched. I jerked my legs toward my body and screamed, "Get away from me! You won't protect us! Nobody will protect us!"

"Ann Marie, I—"

"You remember when you told me that if I made you choose, you would choose him? You remember that?"

The red in her cheeks started to fade. Her lips became a small hyphen beneath her nose. Her hands dropped to her hips then she raised the right one near her face, turning it palm upward and staring at the creases that were supposed to tell her future. I wondered if today was a hash mark on the long line of her life, a little wrinkle marking this event. I imagined her as a small girl who went to the county fair and gave a ticket to the fortune-teller. The old woman skimmed a fingernail across my mother's tiny palm and whispered words: *lovely, happy, joyous.* I bet that little girl, who grew into my mother, never once saw this day coming.

My rage dwindled, and a hollowness filled its place. Quietly, I said, "Why can't you ever choose us?"

She didn't answer me. Some dark, heavy feeling flitted across her face. The corners of her lips eased downward. Her eyelids seemed to sag. She marched into the kitchen, scooped up the telephone receiver, and dialed. After a minute or so, she finally said, "Mom? It's Adele."

I half-turned, my arm flung over the back of the couch. I stared at my mother's back with my mouth agape.

"I know it's been a while," my mother said. "I know—"

She paused for a long time. I could hear her breathe loudly against the mouthpiece. Every so often, she nodded her head while she curled the cord around her index finger. "Mom," she said in a thin voice. "I called to see if you could come stay with us. Just for a little while."

My mother pulled the phone away from her ear, and my grandmother's voice, tinny and loud, screeched through the earpiece. I heard snatches of phrases: *it's been months, haven't heard a peep from you, haven't seen hide nor hair of my grandchildren.* The last thing she said, slowly and clearly, was, *Why don't you call your husband's parents next time you need something?*

My mother answered, "Because they're dead."

Confusion darted across my face. Grandpa Zane's heart had failed while he was driving. My mother was pregnant with Jolene when their car swerved off the road and slammed into a tree, the impact breaking Grandpa Zane's ribs and sending Grandma Rose's forehead crashing against the windshield glass. Grandma Esther, my mother had told me, had been to their funerals.

My mother said, "I wouldn't ask if it weren't important. It'd just be for a little while. Things are hard around here, Mom. That's all. Frank's not feeling well. The girls aren't adjusting. Can't you do this one thing?"

My mother rarely mentioned Grandma Esther, and as long as I'd been alive, I'd only seen her, at most, a couple dozen times. Sometimes, she'd come over for Christmas, and every once in a while, we'd go to her house during the summer. The last time Jolie and I saw her — one hundred and twenty-two long minutes at her kitchen table, sipping lukewarm tea from stained china cups, staring awkwardly at her then our mother then the floor — had been in June, some eight months ago. So it was with a tremendous amount of shock, my mouth gone slack, my eyes opened wide, that I listened to my mother say, "Okay, then, I'll come pick you up by the end of the week."

My mother gently replaced the receiver. She wiped her upper lip with one finger then pushed the hair away from her face. She shuffled toward me, gaze on the floor, and stooped to gather the fallen tomatoes.

"I didn't mean for this ..." I mumbled.

My mother cupped her palm and scooped tomato innards into it. Without looking at me, she said, "It's a done thing, Ann Marie. You were right. Something had to change."

My mother moved into the kitchen and brushed ripped skin, red juice, and green seeds into the sink. She glanced up and stared out the window. "It's just for a little while. Who knows? Maybe it'll actually work out."

"But you don't like Grandma," I said.

She turned toward me with a forced smile straining her face. "She's okay."

"Since when?"

"Since now."

"Daddy won't like it."

"It'll be good for your father."

"Jolie won't like it."

My mother's cheeks reddened. She faced the sink again, her eyes slipping into a soft focus at the tomato juice, red as blood, skidding along the bottom. She mumbled something about a Bible passage she remembered from a long time ago, a verse about a dog slinking back to its vomit. She wondered if she might just be that dog, returning to something foul, begging aid from someone who couldn't help her. She grimaced then spun the tap so water washed the juice down the drain. Loudly, she said, "No. She's coming. That's all there is to it."

IT WAS LATE afternoon on a Friday when my mother pulled into the driveway with Grandma Esther in the front seat, their faces forward, no words flowing between them. Jolie flattened her palms against the edge of her bedroom window and pressed her nose to the glass. I stood beside her while she said, "You just couldn't keep your mouth shut, could you?"

"All I said was she never chose us." When Jolie didn't respond except to curl her fingers more tightly against the frame, I added, "You thought it, too."

"Maybe I was thinking it, but I would've never said it out loud. Now we've gone from bad to worse."

"Who says it'll get worse?"

"Grandma Esther's mean. Mama hates her. Esther plus Adele equals worse."

"How was I supposed to know she was gonna call Grandma Esther?"

"Who else would she turn to?"

"The preacher," I said, grasping at names. "Uncle Tim."

"When was the last time she talked to the preacher?"

I studied the carpet between my feet. "Christmas."

"And Uncle Tim?"

"I don't know."

My sister shoved her index and middle fingers into the air between us. "At least two years. That's how long it's been since the card she sent him for his birthday got returned. He moved and didn't leave a forwarding address. How can you call somebody like that *close*?"

I muttered, "I didn't think she'd call Grandma."

"You should've left it alone. At least Daddy doesn't hurt us anymore."

"He doesn't talk to us either."

Softer, she said, "That's fine with me."

Jolie faced the window again, and we watched my grandmother's thin body leave the passenger's seat of the station wagon. Her face was wrinkled and gray, an almost pasty color, with thick eyebrows, a hard mouth, and wide-rimmed glasses framing two bewildered eyes. Her nose leaked a bit, and she dabbed at it with a white handkerchief.

Soon, the hinges of the side door squawked, and frigid air blew inside. "We're here," my mother called then dropped an enormous brown suitcase, like an exclamation point to finish her sentence, on the floor by her feet.

January 1971

ON NEW YEAR'S Day, my mother kicked Grandma Esther out of our house.

For nearly the entire year since our grandmother had moved in, Jolie spent mornings and afternoons hiding in the cellar with her charcoal pencils and pads of paper. In the early evenings, she walked the edge of the road, going north for a half-mile or so to see Patrick O'Flannery, the same boy who'd gone with us all those years ago for ice cream.

A few weeks after Grandma Esther arrived, Jolie had stolen a pair of scissors up to her bedroom, sat on the edge of the bed, stared out the window at the snow falling lightly to the ground, and sheared strand after strand of her long hair until her scalp was dotted with light-blonde tufts. I leaned against her doorjamb and when she was finished, the scissors dangling from her fingers, I asked, "Why'd you do that?"

She shrugged then reached near her ankles and grabbed a handful of hair in her fist. She thrust it toward me and said, "You have it. What do I need it for?"

At dinner, my mother's mouth was a wide circle as her hands danced across my sister's scalp, gently touching the clipped, broken ends of her hair.

Over the months, I had learned to stay in my bedroom, curled on the floor near the closet, surrounding myself with books. I would leave the bedroom door cracked just slightly so I could hear the creak of the stairs and smell the faint stale odor that clung to my grandmother, preceding her wherever she went. Quietly, I would shut my book and scoot inside the closet, hiding behind a wall of clothes, breathing light and low, until she moved on down the hall and up the stairs into the attic where my mother had shoved everything to one side to make the other half my grandmother's bedroom.

My father would give Grandma Esther an enormous berth, waking early and staying outside nearly all day then waiting at least half an hour after the light in the attic went dark before he stepped a foot back into the house. There were days that I didn't see him except through my bedroom window. For a stretch of weeks, I never heard him utter even one word. My mother had wanted her mother to act as a buffer, and that part of her plan seemed to be working. After my grandmother came, no one in my family spent much time together in the same room. But Grandma Esther's being there did nothing to help the main problem — my father's sickness couldn't be contained: he was distant and moving further away every day. And her presence created another rift: Jolene scampered away every day, plunging herself into distractions, and rarely spoke to me anymore.

My mother seemed stiff and watchful all the time. She blushed, her face a gorgeous scarlet, nearly every time she was in the same room with my grandmother. She stumbled through words — pausing, groaning, trying again — each time she spoke. When I entered a room, she stared at me with a kind of longing in her eyes, like she just wished we could go back in time before Grandma Esther came, before my father got sick.

To add to all that, my grandmother nipped at cooking sherry, sipping a bit here and a bit there until, at the end of the day, nearly a full bottle would be emptied. By evening, her old eyes were glassy, the right one milky with a cataract, and when she looked at you, you weren't sure if she saw you or not. Often after dinner, when only a few drops remained in the bottle, she would slump on the couch in the living room and mumble on about Grandpa Joseph, who died long before we were born. Sometimes, she'd lean toward the armrest and plant a kiss with a loud smacking sound in the air where his face might have been. Other times, she'd talk to that empty space, asking how his day had been, did he miss her, had he noticed how big the children had gotten. About a month after she moved in, Jolene and I started to avoid her entirely when she began demanding that we say hello to our dead grandfather then motioned us with broad sweeps of her arms to give him a big hug.

The demise of my grandmother's stay started on Christmas morning. With all of us in one room for the first time since Thanksgiving — my mother and grandmother on the couch, my father leaning against the wall near the kitchen, Jolie and me sitting cross-legged on the carpet beside the tree — we ripped open gifts from Grandma Esther as she watched with a cup of cold coffee in her hand.

My mother lifted a beige blouse from the gift wrap. The armpits were stained the faintest yellow, and a white tag dangled from a white string pinned to the collar. She stared at the tag, the undeniable sign of the Goodwill in town, and her arms sagged. It said, *10 cents*. Chin quivering, she barked a quick sob before shoving the back of her hand into her mouth to stifle it.

Jolie unwrapped a pair of brown corduroy pants, the knees worn thin. The white tag through a belt loop said, *50 cents*.

Grandma Esther smiled. "Do you like those, dear?"

Jolie raised them toward the empty side of the couch and said dully, "Maybe Grandpa Joe would like them better."

My grandmother's face dimmed. Her lips clamped together. She lowered her coffee cup against her thigh and looked at the empty space beside her then back at Jolene.

I draped a sweater at least two sizes too small across my thighs. It was blue and brown with a stiff fabric teddy bear sewed on the front. Its white tag said, *50 cents*.

My grandmother pulled a wad of tissues from her dress pocket and crimped them in her fist. In a quiet voice, her eyes staring down toward her lap, she said, "The lady at the Goodwill said you could bring everything back if you don't like it. She said just make sure I leave the tags on."

My mother's face pinched up, and a strangled sound gurgled from her throat.

"For heaven's sakes, what's the matter?" my grandmother said.

My father leaned against the wall behind the couch with his arms crossed over his chest. Thick with prescription drugs, he said, "It's the used gifts, Esther. Always getting your kids used gifts."

My grandmother stiffened at the sound of his voice. She placed her coffee cup, its rim stained with deep red lipstick, on the end table and craned her neck toward my father. "What would you know about that?"

My father stepped toward the couch, his hand braced against the wall for support. "Aren't they worth more to you than that? Doesn't anybody matter enough that you'd buy them a little something they wanted instead of some cheap thing you picked up at the Goodwill?"

My grandmother's black look moved from him to my mother. "*Some* of us don't have money growing on trees. *Some* of us have a fixed income."

"You still buy booze," my mother answered so softly I nearly didn't hear it.

My grandmother grabbed her coffee mug and drank deeply. Afterward, she wiped her lips with the ball of tissues in her hand. She glared at my mother and said, "What did you say to me?"

"Booze. You always had enough money to get drunk."

"I am not drunk."

"Maybe not yet. But in a few minutes, a few hours ..." My mother reached across the cushions for the cup in my grandmother's hand. "Let me taste that coffee you're drinking. I bet it's laced with more than just sugar."

My grandmother snatched the cup away, and light-colored coffee sloshed onto her green dress. "I'm your mother. *You* don't tell me how to live my life. I came here to help you, remember? You're still *my* daughter. You'll still treat me with respect."

My mother laughed then glanced at me. "Ann Marie and I just had that same conversation before you even came here. In fact, it's the reason you're here at all."

My grandmother's eyes flitted around the room and her arm jerked wildly, index finger jabbing toward each of us. Her stale smell wafted through the air. "You ought to be happy you got presents at all. Ungrateful, you are. Spoiled. Some kids don't have a thing. Some kids have to wake up and stare at the empty floor underneath the tree. Some don't even have trees, but just a piece of mistletoe on the radiator. You're ungrateful. All of you. Ungrateful wretches."

My father moved slowly toward the couch until he towered over my grandmother, his wide hands gripping her bony shoulders. "You don't talk about my family that way, Esther. You treated your kids bad. You won't treat my kids bad."

My grandmother squealed at his touch and jerked away from him. She glared at my mother. "I did the best I could!" When my mother said nothing, she shouted at my father, "*You're* the reason I'm here. *You're* the one treating your kids bad."

My father shriveled as if he'd been punched in the gut. He looked at me sitting on the floor then Jolene nearer the tree. A weak smile pinched up the corners of his mouth. He turned and, with his hand skimming against the wall, limped from the room.

"Wait!" my mother called.

"She's right," my father said, pausing with his arm out and his back to us. "Can't argue with that."

We finished Christmas day in relative silence. My father disappeared outside. My mother vanished into her bedroom, shutting the door quietly behind her. Jolene dressed then trudged through the snow, plodding down the driveway then alongside the road to Patrick's house. My grandmother stayed on the couch for a while, her stunned face gazing past the Christmas tree and out the front window to a red cardinal chittering atop a branch of the buckeye tree. After a while, she heaved herself up with a grunt, her coffee mug still clasped in her hand, and shuffled past me, going up the stairs to her bedroom in the attic.

Sitting by myself next to the Christmas tree, its white lights blinking on and off every so often, I listened to my grandmother turn on the small black-and-white television she'd brought with her. High-decibel words about a parade floated down the staircase. Soon, my grandmother's voice joined them as she commented to my dead grandfather, "How beautiful! Think of the craftsmanship it must've taken to make such beautiful floats. And the time! Heavens, it must've taken so much time!"

I pushed my gifts under the tree, stood up, and walked into the foyer. I stared at the closed door of my mother's bedroom for a minute before, still in my pajamas, I pulled on a pair of boots and my navy peacoat. I opened the side door, and cold air blasted across my face, snow pelted my cheeks.

I thought of going to a friend's house, of telling the truth to anyone who might listen. But then my mother's words from a long time ago echoed in my head, *Our dirty laundry is nobody else's business. People here ... they like to talk. We need to, well, not tell anybody else about what happened. I don't want it to be hard for us to live in this town.* And my focus shifted instead to the footprints in the snow. I followed them, and a few minutes later, I found my father tinkering near the busted green tractor in the front of the barn.

I closed the barn door softly behind me and leaned against the wood. My father's short hair had gone gray near the temples. His muscles had weakened. He gritted his teeth, and I noticed black gaps where a few were missing. Over the past year, his frame had gotten heavy, fat hanging in folds off his bones. His jeans were too small, a roll of flesh hanging over the waistband and pushing out the flannel shirt he wore. He gripped a wrench in his right hand and stared at a bolt near the tractor's metal seat.

Beyond my father, six stalls lined one side of the barn and five the other side, even though the horses had been gone for years. Some of the windowpanes high up in the stalls were broken, and cool air seeped in through the cracks. Cobwebs stuck fast in nearly every corner. Lime caked against the dirt. I was a few months shy of sixteen years old, but the memory slammed into me as if I were ten again: the gun barrel pressed against his forehead and his words, *Sing me a song, angel, or I'll pull the trigger.* My hands quaked, and I flattened them against my thighs. My bladder felt full and heavy. I thought of whirling around and running toward the house. My legs started to inch backward. But my father's deep voice stopped me. Rolling a bolt in the palm of his hand, looking at it and not me, he said, "What'd you need?"

My eyes darted around. I stumbled through words. "I just ... uh ... well, I wanted you to know it was ... um ... nice that you ... stood up for us."

He looked up at the sound of my voice, eyes sliding to the right and left of me, searching for someone else. "You're not Adele."

"No."

"I thought you were Adele."

I stood quietly with my hands in my pockets, fingers squeezing a ball of lint shoved in the bottom.

"Can you get her?" he finally asked.

"You can talk to me without her," I said.

He harrumphed and turned his gaze back at his hands, to the bolt in one and the wrench in the other. He started to fiddle with the tractor's seat again.

"Daddy, please ..."

He stopped and, not looking at me, said, "It's not safe for you here."

"Why?"

"You have to go."

"I don't want to go."

He loosened his fingers, and the wrench and bolt landed with soft thuds against the dirt floor. Without another word, he wandered away from me, past the empty horse stalls and down the narrow corridor that led to a large space where hay used to be stored. For a while, I heard nothing except the occasional creak of wood as the wind struck against the roof. Every so often, some unseen rodent rustled and scuffled about.

I waited, ten minutes, maybe fifteen. I shifted my weight and stamped the melting snow from my boots. I didn't know whether to stay or go. My head screamed, *run*. My gut said softly, *stay*. I walked partway across the floor and stared into the half-light and shadows that played around the corridor. I moved sideways until I planted my hand against the door of a stall. The air was heavy with the smells of old manure and moldered hay. I started to feel dizzy and sick.

In the dimness, I saw my father's silhouette. Kneeling on the dirt floor, he clutched his head in his hands. I took a step forward, and he screamed into his lap. His voice rose in pitch, his chin moving upward, his mouth howling at the ceiling. I froze, my fingers curling against the stall to hold myself up. My head chanted, *run, run, run*. My knees felt doughy, like they might not hold my weight much longer. In the room where my father knelt, curling into himself again, weeping into his lap, sunlight spilled through a window near the rafters and onto his rounded back. I eased myself backward then slipped quietly out the barn's front door. I moved toward the house, still hearing my father's piercing cries in my head.

An hour or so later, my boots and jacket leaving puddles on the foyer's brown carpet, I waited by the stove for the kettle to boil. My mother plunked two mugs on the counter. She pulled a tin of black tea from the cupboard and slowly scooped leaves into the tea ball.

Watching the stove, I said, "How long's she going to stay?"

My mother gently closed the cabinet door. "Not much longer now, I don't imagine."

"Will you ask her to leave?"

"I should've never asked her to come."

The kettle whistled and I said, "Daddy stuck up for us."

A slight smile softened her face as she dropped the tea ball into the boiling water. "Yes, he did. He loves you, you know? Maybe he doesn't always show it, but he does."

"Maybe he'll get better now."

"Yes," she said. "Maybe he will."

For the next week, my grandmother hid in her room and drank. When she heard anyone within earshot, she started to grumble about how ungrateful we were and how miserable she was. My mother ignored her, so Jolene and I did the same. My father spent most of his time puttering around the barn. Life went back to the way it had been before Christmas when all of us avoided one another.

Then New Year's Eve came, and my grandmother plopped herself on the living room couch with a bottle of sherry clutched in one hand. She watched the countdown on television, the ball dropping while her eyes glazed over, and got so drunk that she fell onto the floor. In the first few minutes of 1971, my father and I carried my grandmother to bed, and my mother cried with her face buried in her lap as confetti rained down on the streets of New York. Jolene blew on a plastic horn then said, "Happy New Year."

"Like a dog to its vomit," my mother said, her eyes swollen and red. "This is my fault. I'll take care of it."

After dawn broke, I awoke to the sound of my grandmother wailing. I rushed up the stairwell to the attic and found her brown suitcase open on the floor near a metal rack of clothes while my mother stood nearby, tearing items from their hangers.

"Things never change, Mother. I thought that maybe after all this time ..." She jerked her arm, and a white blouse fluttered into the suitcase. "But things never change, do they?"

My grandmother, her hair mashed down on one side and her skin blotchy and red, shrieked, "What're you doing?"

"You're leaving."

"But it's so early." My grandmother reached over to the nightstand, pulled the alarm clock close to her face, then put it back. From the doorway, I could see a bottle of sherry tucked between the folds of her blanket. "It's barely seven o'clock, Adele."

"Yes."

A few feet above my grandmother was a small, round window. Sunlight spilled past the sides of the shade, and she glanced at the light, grimaced, then pressed a hand to her head. "Oh, that hurts."

"You got drunk again," my mother said, tossing two dresses and a pair of nylons rolled into a tight ball toward the suitcase.

"It was New Year's."

"You passed out."

"No, I must've fallen asleep."

My mother stopped with a girdle in her hand. "Even your excuses don't change."

My grandmother whined, "What're you doing with my clothes?"

My mother heaved the girdle at the suitcase. "Like I said, you're leaving."

Grandma Esther peered over the edge of the bed and saw a mound of clothes draped over the sides of her suitcase. "But you're wrinkling them! They need to be folded. Do you know how long it will take me to iron them out?"

My mother kept moving, her hands alternating between the clothes rack and the suitcase. Blouses, slacks, and a skirt with a rose embroidered on it sailed through the air. A pair of white bloomers floated down, missing the mark and landing on the floor.

Grandma Esther squealed, "You're soiling my things!"

My mother spun around, a blue dress clenched in her fist. "Is that all you can say? Really, is that it?"

My grandmother frowned. She primped at her bluish-gray hair, fluffing the strands that were matted against her scalp. Afterward, she licked her index finger and rubbed at the dried spittle crusted on the edge of her mouth.

"I'm waiting," my mother said.

"What in heaven's name do you want me to say, Adele? You're acting crazy."

"I'm not crazy. Finally, Mother, I'm acting sane."

"Sane is not throwing my things in a suitcase and kicking me out on New Year's Day." She shot a look toward the stairs. "Is it, Ann Marie?"

My mother seemed surprised that I was there. "Leave her out of this."

"Doesn't she have a say if she wants her grandmother to go? Wouldn't it be better for her if I stayed? Even if *you* don't want me." She smiled at me, eyes wide, face hopeful. When I didn't answer but just looked from her to my mother and back again, my grandmother blared, "Ungrateful!"

My mother yanked the last piece of clothing from its hanger. "You reap what you sow," she said, tossing a faded red button-down sweater toward the floor. "Isn't that what you were always telling Tim and Peter and me?"

My grandmother pulled the blankets to her neck. "I never sowed ungratefulness."

My mother moved to the pine dresser beside the window and gathered up bottles of perfume and jars of lotion. She tossed one after another toward the suitcase. "You were grateful for the bottles of wine. You weren't grateful for us kids."

"You don't know how hard it was to raise kids. What do you know about raising kids years ago?"

My mother whirled around and pointed at me. "There's one. And there's another downstairs." She yanked the shade and it flapped upward. Squash-colored light fell into the room, and my grandmother hauled the blankets above her eyes.

"Oh, Adele!" she said. "My head!"

My mother jabbed a finger toward the window. "There's also one in the ground."

My eyes and mouth opened wide. Up to that point, the only person in my family to ever mention my dead brother — and even then, I hadn't necessarily believed her — had been Jolene.

"It was different back then," my grandmother whispered behind the blanket. "Harder."

"Oh, bullshit!" my mother said as she jerked open a drawer full of paired socks and scooped them between her hands. She shuffled toward the suitcase, spotted me at the edge of the room, and said, "Marie, honey, close your mouth. You're not out catching flies."

My grandmother dropped the blanket and beat a bony fist against the mattress. Color flared in her cheeks. "*You* don't know what it's like to be married to a man who won't spend his money on anything but liquor. *You* don't know what it's like to have him choose booze over heat. *You* don't have any idea how hard it was to make ends meet. I *had* to buy you kids presents from the secondhand store. I *had* no choice."

My mother dumped the balled socks on top of the suitcase, most of them rolling down the pile of clothes and bouncing onto the floor. She shook her head slowly. Her empty hands fluttered around her waist. "You always managed to buy your booze, though, didn't you, Mom? You always managed to have a bender even when there was nothing but moldy bread and a single potato left to eat."

My grandmother squinted toward the window, sunlight crashing off the snow gathered on the sill. She whimpered, raised a hand to her temple, and closed her eyes.

"Tell me I'm wrong, Mom."

My mother waited for a minute, sighed, then kneeled on the floor beside the suitcase. She stuffed my grandmother's things wherever they would fit and slammed the lid shut. At the sound of the latches snapping closed, my grandmother said, "I don't have anything else to say. You don't like your presents, you take them back."

My mother started to drag the suitcase from the room. Under her breath, she said, "Why don't you go get drunk? That's what you seem to know best. You can spend money on cooking sherry but not on your grandkids, not on your own daughter."

My grandmother slid her pale legs over the side of the mattress then tossed the covers so they fluttered and settled around her ankles. The cotton nightgown she wore molded against the strange shape of her body — thin chest, thick belly, wide hips, spindly legs. Her face lost what color it had. She begged, "Don't make me go!"

My mother hesitated for a moment. She gripped the suitcase's handle tighter between her hands and said quietly, "You'll do fine without us. You always have." She picked up the suitcase again and added, "Ann Marie, honey, get out of the way."

I backed down the stairs.

"She'll grow up ungrateful," my grandmother yelled. "You're teaching her a bad thing."

My mother didn't say a word.

"You're mad at me for growing up bad, but let me tell you a thing, you had it good compared to some. You may not like my drinking, but at least you've got a mother. Some kids didn't even have that."

Without speaking, my mother banged the suitcase down the stairs and disappeared from my grandmother's view. After that, Grandma Esther talked in a voice much too loud about how life was better than my mother remembered it, how you shouldn't hold grudges forever, how she did the best she knew how. My grandmother paused here and there, but my mother didn't answer; instead, she carted the suitcase through the hallway, dragging it a few feet then letting it thunk against the floor.

My grandmother hiked up the shrillness of her voice. "Did you at least leave me something to wear?"

My mother stopped at the edge of the stairs to the living room, popped the latches, and yanked out a wadded white blouse, a wrinkled blue skirt, and a balled pair of nylons. "Take these to your grandmother, Ann Marie."

Hearing my mother's voice, my grandmother hollered, "It wasn't that I didn't love you and Timmy and Peter. There was just so much yelling. It didn't seem like anybody could hear me unless I was yelling." She sighed before adding, "Peter's dead now."

My mother's hands shook as she slammed the lid back closed.

My grandmother whined, "Peter's dead, and Timmy and you don't want me."

"Take them now, Ann Marie." My mother hefted the suitcase against her body and started to haul it downstairs.

"I couldn't help that I didn't know better. What did I know about having kids? All of you begging for my time. Always needing something." When I got into the attic, my grandmother was wrenching her nightgown in her fists, yanking and stretching at the pink cotton. She stared at me, at her clothes in my hands, and said in a quiet voice, "What about me? What about what I need? Nobody ever asked about that. Kids are born and right away they start taking. First from your breast, then from your wallet, and finally all you got left is a hollow bone where once there was some meat."

I bit my tongue to keep from talking, feeling the thick flesh of it between my teeth, and dropped her clothes on the dresser.

"Don't nobody bargain for that," my grandmother said.

My mother grunted loudly as she dropped the heavy suitcase on the living room floor.

"It was your father's fault, you know!" Grandma Esther yelled past me. "It was him who got me started drinking. I was never a drinker until I married him. Had to start drinking for every occasion. Then after a while, I found I couldn't do without it. If it wasn't for your father, I wouldn't have been like that. Things might've been different. You know everybody thought your father was a saint. Thought he walked on water, they did. But I knew the truth. I knew about the drinking and the screaming and the marks he used to leave on my back. Nobody else could see those. Not even you, Adele."

Feet shuffled, the suitcase thunked, a loud grunting noise came again.

My grandmother stumbled over to me at the edge of the stairwell, her face shriveled and sad. "Why doesn't she get angry at him? Why doesn't she do that for a change? Instead of always being angry at me."

My mother's faint reply: "He's dead."

My grandmother shouted down the steps, "I'm the only one left to blame, is that it? Can't get mad at him, so get mad at me?"

My mother's rhythm — heave, shuffle, slide, and grunt — started again.

"I can't do anything about the past, Adele. When are you going to learn that? I can't help that I wasn't the mother you wanted. I was the mother you got. Life doesn't always give you what you want." My grandmother paused and pursed her mouth. Her eyes were hard as flint. She grabbed the railing, yelling, "Do you hear me?"

I rushed down the stairs, arriving in the foyer just as my mother scooted out the front door in her slippers and robe. She stared up at the gray sky while fat, wet snowflakes swirled around her. "There's never a quick fix," she mumbled. "I've prayed. I've fasted. I've begged. What more do you want?"

On the second floor landing, my grandmother shouted, "What? What are you saying?"

"Frank came home alive but sick. My mother is no help. The girls are hurting. You're supposed to help us." She dropped the suitcase into the snow and shook her clenched fist toward the sky. "Why else are you there?"

It was strange to hear my mother speak to God. When Jolene and I were younger, she'd send us off to Vacation Bible School for a week during the summer, not so much to be religious as to get us out of her hair. Otherwise, she'd take us to church services on Christmas and Easter where she would hunch in a pew and beg favor, first from the preacher with her fingers grasping her heaving chest, and second from God with her head bowed and her hands woven together. She would say words like, "Can't you change him? Fix what's wrong? Make things better?" The whole time my father hunkered on the couch, jaw set, fingers clutching the armrest, refusing to come. Years ago, on the Easter after the television showed a bound Viet Cong captain being hauled to a street corner and shot point-blank in the head, I sat in the front seat of the car, suffering in my starched dress, and asked, "Well, how come Daddy's not coming?"

"Your daddy won't go to church."

"Well, how come?"

"Daddy doesn't believe in God."

"How come we have to go?"

From the backseat, Jolie chimed in, "Yeah?"

"You hush," my mother said to the rearview mirror. "And you," she said to me, her skin gone a bit paler, her fingers gripped tightly around the steering wheel, "Just because somebody doesn't believe a thing doesn't make that thing not true. God's real whether Daddy thinks so or not, and we're going to worship."

"How come we don't go every Sunday then?"

My mother stared out the windshield, past a bug that had died in a quarter-sized splatter, and never did answer.

We never talked much about God. I rarely heard her pray. So it was with some surprise that I watched her drag the suitcase across the driveway, carving a groove in the snow, with her face angled upward as she shouted, cursed, and finally dropped the suitcase, sat on its edge, curled her face toward her lap then covered it with her hands, and wept at heaven. A few minutes later, her eyes red and swollen, she stood up, wiped her face with her sleeve, and started dragging the suitcase toward the garage beside the barn.

Jolie, in pajamas and her short hair all cowlicked, padded into the foyer. My grandmother, still in her nightgown, her clothes forgotten in a heap in the attic, came shortly after her. Shoulders slumped, mouth pulled into a frown, my grandmother said, "Where's your mother going?"

"To the car," I said.

"Why?"

"You're leaving."

"I don't want to leave," she said.

"Mama's mad."

"But it's New Year's Day. That's no way to start the New Year."

"You're just like the presents," Jolie said.

"What?" Grandma Esther said.

"She doesn't like you, so she's taking you back."

OVER THE MONTHS that my grandmother lived with us, each member of my family had settled themselves into a pattern: my father dodged everyone; Jolene hid in the cellar or at Patrick's house; my mother slipped into a quiet, sullen state; I snuck away by myself with a book. After Grandma Esther left, we kept those habits, growing further away from each other a little more every day.

I DIDN'T HEAR about my grandmother again until four months later when a telegram from my uncle announced the heart attack that killed her. As a kid, I believed that somehow I had nurtured along her death. It was true I had hated living with her, but being at her funeral, seeing her stiff, lifeless body in a casket, swamped me with such guilt that I didn't eat for three days. For months afterward, thinking about her would cause my chest to seize up and sharp twinges of pain to radiate out from the hard knot above my pubic bone. My temples would pound, and I'd have to lie down.

Jolene, though, seemed oddly detached. "She's better off," she said to me one August evening at dusk as we sat on the porch shelling peanuts. "She doesn't have to be here anymore."

I glanced at her, my chest tightening. "With us?"

She stared across the front lawn and popped a peanut in her mouth. "On this planet."

"Why do you say that?"

"I hate it here. She's lucky not to have to be here anymore. God did her a favor."

I crushed a peanut shell under my palm and started to count the pieces it made. Pain chugged along inside my head. "But you have Patrick ..."

My sister watched the setting sun purple the horizon like some terrible bruise and whispered, "Yeah."

We stayed like that for a few minutes, me saying quiet numbers to myself, Jolene staring across the grass toward the dirt road while a small spasm shook the fingers of her right hand. A roaring headache began to knock against my skull. A couple of times, I opened my mouth to utter something but couldn't manage to say it. The hinges of the screen door squawked and our mother told us dinner was ready before she disappeared back into the house. Jolene moved to stand up. I grabbed her wrist, a great fire burning in my head, and mumbled, "I love you."

She smiled weakly at me and said, "I love you too, Marie. But that's probably not enough."

June 1972

ONE SATURDAY AT breakfast, my mother burrowed her thumbs into the middle of an orange and tore it in two. Chunks of the peel rocked on top of the table as she sectioned one piece, her thumbnail plucking off the fibery veins, and tucked it into her mouth. She chewed slowly, swallowed, then glanced across the table at me. In the pale sunlight, I noticed the crow's feet in the skin around her eyes, the lines of gray that streaked her hair. She said, "I'm taking your father for a drive."

I picked at the toast in front of me and asked, "Where?"

"I don't know." She sipped at her coffee before adding, "We need some fresh air. Air fresher than this town has to offer."

A dollop of grape jelly lodged under my fingernail. I sucked it off my finger then asked quietly, "You're not going to drop him off someplace, are you?"

She smiled sadly. "No. It's too late for that now anyhow. We just need a break from the war and the napalm strikes and the dead soldiers."

"But the television's off," I said.

She rested her coffee cup on the table and picked up a piece of orange rind, smoothing it flat against her palm. "This house seems to press on him, Ann Marie. 'Smothering,' he tells me. So we're going away today." Softer, she added, "We'll go somewhere light. Somewhere with flowers."

From the porch, I watched the taillights of my father's rust-eaten Chevy truck linger at the end of the driveway. Exhaust spilled past the planks of bolted-on plywood that made the truck's bed. My mother slid out of the driver's side to pitch a handful of letters into the mailbox and raise the faded red flag. There was a bounce in her step that hadn't been there for so long. It made me wonder, as I hurried down the steps and onto the grass, dew glazing my bare feet, if she really was planning to leave him somewhere. Waving my hands wildly in the air, I was suddenly afraid that I might not see my father again.

My mother had already sunk into the driver's seat, slammed the door, and ground the gears into first. I stutter-stepped forward, hands fluttering above my head, as they rumbled onto the road. They drove north, beyond the pine-tree windbreak, and out of my view. I stopped and let my hands fall against my sides. I stared at the dust churning, watching until it settled back down. I saw a blue jay fly across the road and perch on the low, sagging arc of a telephone wire. Behind me, the screen door banged and my sister's thin voice followed right after.

"What're you doing?" she said.

I turned around, cupping a hand against my forehead to shade my eyes. "They went for a drive."

"Yeah." She sat on the porch swing, one foot folded underneath her, the other kicking against the wood floor. Sunlight fluttered across her face as she rocked in and out of the shadows. I could see how thin she'd gotten. Her hip bones jutted from beneath her cotton pants. Her chest and her cheeks looked sunken and hollow. Dark smudges appeared under her eyes. After a time, she added, "So?"

I climbed a few porch steps, the wood bowing with my weight, then paused and leaned against the railing. "I was just watching them go."

The porch swing creaked on its metal chains as my sister replied, "You're getting crazy in your old age."

"Seventeen's hardly old."

She jammed the ball of her foot against the floorboards, stopping the swing. She cut her eyes to the buckeye tree off to the left in the front yard. "I can't imagine being seventeen."

"What're you talking about?"

She shook her head and glanced at me. "I'm going to see Patrick."

"Jolene," I said, fingers curling around the railing. "What's the matter?"

She shrugged and looked over at the buckeye tree again.

"You spend a lot of time with him," I said.

"Better than here."

She unfastened the top three buttons of her white blouse, and I saw a thin, gold chain hanging against her pale throat. Between the small swell of her breasts lay a thick-banded class ring.

"His?" I asked.

"Uh-huh." She buttoned her shirt and slid her leg out from underneath her.

"When'd he give it to you?"

"A couple weeks ago."

"How come you didn't say anything?"

She shrugged again. Softly, she said, "It was something between us."

Feeling insignificant in her life, I blurted, "Are you going to marry him?"

She touched the ring through the cotton of her shirt and nodded. "He touches me and it doesn't hurt. He sees me when I stand next to him. He talks to me as if I'm really there." After a time, she whispered more to herself than me, "We've slept together."

Low, near my pubic bone, I felt the first real twinge of loss. I had always wanted a sister with whom I could share everything, and I understood, as I watched her stare into the middle distance, that our relationship was evaporating like so much water on a hot griddle. I asked, "When?"

"June, last year."

My face felt hot and sticky. I could feel the prickle of sweat in my armpits. "Why didn't you tell me?"

"I didn't tell anybody."

"But I'm your sister."

"I don't know, Marie." She moved to the edge of the porch stairs and sat down. Sunlight radiated off her light-colored hair, surrounding her like a halo. "It was just something Patrick and I needed for ourselves."

I wanted to touch her. I wanted to feel the heat of her against me because it had been so many years since we huddled in her bed, me whispering in her ear, her body trembling against mine. I wanted my little sister back: her laugh, her smile, the smell of citrus on her hair. I wanted to feel the soft, rhythmic beat of her heart. A strange chirping sound spilled out of my mouth as I lurched forward, hands flailing, in a graceless, weak-kneed way toward her. She drew away from me, her behind scooting backward on the porch, her legs pulling into her chest. I stopped and a winded feeling, like getting punched off-guard, hollowed out my chest.

"We're sisters," I whined.

"You don't want to touch me," she said.

"Why not?"

Her eyes wandered to the buckeye tree. Faintly, she said, "That's where I buried it."

"Buried what?"

She wreathed her arms around her legs and, chin quivering, started to rock slowly back and forth. "The condom broke."

"You buried a condom?" I said.

"No. The condom broke, and I got pregnant. And we knew ..." She paused, breathed in then sighed out. "The minute it broke, we just knew."

I watched her thighs mold against her flat belly and said, "But you're not pregnant now." The hairs on my arms stood on end as it dawned on me what lay beneath the tree. I whispered, "You buried the baby?"

She ran the flat of one palm against the floorboards in tight, small circles. "Last August. I had all those cramps and all that blood. Then there was a piece of Patrick and me floating on the bed sheets. I couldn't bear the thought of washing it down the drain. So I scooped up what I could and buried it beneath the buckeye." Softer, she added, "The buckeye was always safe."

"You miscarried?"

She nodded. "It was just two months old."

I moved toward her again, my hand brushing her bare foot. "For Godsakes, Jolie, why didn't you say something?"

At my touch, she scrambled backward, pushing with her hands and feet until she was a yard away. She stood up and, staring down at me, said, "Grandma Esther was dead. There was so much else keeping everyone busy. What difference was it going to make? The baby was gone. I'm sorry I didn't tell you. I guess we should've been closer than that."

She turned away from me, and an image blazed into my head of a rock skipping across a pond, skimming over the surface, and you can count the big moments in its life, one, two, three, and then there's the last one where it sinks beneath the water and isn't seen again. My sister's hand touched the screen door, ready to disappear into the house, and the image of that sunken stone wouldn't let me go. I barked, "Is there anything else you want to tell me?"

She padded across the threshold and let the door slam shut behind her. Through the mesh of the screen, she said, "You ever feel like you're just a small thing that doesn't matter?

Like a smudge beside the main point?" Her voice trailed off. When I didn't say anything, she added, "I feel like that a lot. I'm going to Patrick's now. I'll be back later."

After Jolie left, I walked through the quiet house. In the living room, I touched the mantle of the fireplace, smearing a line through the dust. In the bathroom, I fingered a bar of lavender-scented soap. In Jolie's bedroom, I brushed against the leaves of a fern near the windowsill. In the attic, where Grandma Esther had stayed, I ran my palm against one wall. In the stillness of everything, it occurred to me, as I blew dirt from my fingertips, how little space I, myself, took up in everyone's lives.

In the kitchen, I slid my hands into the sink under a cool stream of water. I raised my head and saw out the window that one of the cellar doors was flung open. I hadn't been down there in years, but within a minute, I was outside on the grass, peering down the stairs into the darkness. The wooden stairs creaked under my weight. I ran my fingernails along the wall, leaving small, evenly spaced trails in the dirt. The closer I got to the bottom, the thicker and heavier the air seemed to be. By the last step, I began to feel suffocated, darkness plugging my eyes, nose, and mouth.

I waited for my sight to adjust to the dimness and breathed in the smell of my sister, peppermint and black licorice. Soon, the objects along the walls became more than just shadows, and the smile on my face faded like brightly colored curtains too long in the sun. My gut clamped down, and I scurried over to the corner where I remembered the supply box to be, searching for the propane lantern.

In the light, I saw that two entire walls and nearly half of a third were covered with artwork. I thought of my sister sitting cross-legged in the dimness, a huge pad of paper balanced on her knees, a charcoal pencil honed to a thin point, her right elbow flying as color spilled onto the page. Some of the pages I recognized from our day together so many years ago. Those were yellowed, their edges frayed and curled. There were many others I'd never seen, the paper in various stages of decay.

Nearly every picture held an image of my father. First as a stick figure, all straight black lines with a circle for a head. As her hand grew steadier and her tools more refined, she drew him with a sharpened pencil in profile, then full on. The detail was so precise that even the lines making his face look enraged and hateful came through the tip of her lead. I shuffled along the wall, following the images with the lantern held out in front of me, and saw the times in Jolie's life where one thing or another caught her attention, and my father made appearances in landscapes, a bowl of fruit, the demon in a drawing of angels. For a while, after she'd read some book of fantasy, an ogre held my father's face. A few pictures later, a character from the book slew that ogre/father, slicing its head from its body, and afterward, danced in victory, swinging the severed head by its hair. In some of the drawings, Jolie had sketched herself, a figure I knew to be her even though it was faceless except for X's where its eyes should've been. It was almost always broken in some way. Other drawings held our mother, a blur in the background with no eyes, no ears, and no hands, a figure of no help to anyone.

My light came upon a circle dug into the dirt near the bottom corner of one wall. The day we were in the cellar together, Jolie had asked me to be still and had drawn my face. She hadn't shown it to me then, but I saw that yellowed picture now in the center of that circle. There was also a picture of her and Patrick at the county fair, a Ferris wheel in the background. There was a pencil drawing of my dead brother, the same image as the photograph tucked away in my father's footlocker. Last, next to the baby's face, there was a Bible verse on a piece of notebook paper, the blue lines smeared from the damp.

I squatted down, my fingers following the outline of the circle, and it occurred to me that Jolene had dug a kind of moat around the good things in her life. I brushed my fingertips along the words of the verse, my mouth moving as I read silently.

Love is patient, love is kind
It does not envy, it does not boast,
*   it is not proud*
It is not rude, it is not self-seeking
It is not easily angered,
*   it keeps no record of wrongs*
Love does not delight in evil
But rejoices with the truth
It always protects, always trusts,
*   always hopes*
Always perseveres
Love never fails.

In the supply box, I found a blue pen and a scrap of red paper not much bigger than a postcard. I scribbled my own note to Jolene, the phrase she'd said to me all those years ago, *Faith as small as a mustard seed can move mountains.* I slipped my note under one of the pushpins that held the drawing of my face, patted it with my hand, and stood up.

On my way out of the cellar, a swatch of brown paper caught my eye. I raised the lantern and saw my future life, the one I'd wished for myself when I was eleven. In the center, below a smattering of lopsided blue stars, was Jolie's smooth, round seed, small as a sweet pea. It was the seed she had carried with her for so long, the one she used as a measure of her faith. I didn't understand, then, why it was stuck fast to my collage.

I thought of adding something to my picture, even raised the pen a notch higher and poised it over the paper. I stood like that for a minute, then two, but couldn't think of anything to say. I dropped the pen and the lantern back into the supply box, crossed the cellar, and climbed slowly up the stairs into the fresh air. The door clattered shut behind me, slivers of rotted wood showering the grass at my feet.

DUSK DARKENED THE sky and Jolene was still at Patrick's house when my father's truck — the passenger's side wheel rim eaten through by rust, a caved-in dent in the hood where long ago he'd sideswiped a tree — trundled up the driveway. Near the barn, my mother laughed and dangled her short legs out the door. She scooted to the edge of the seat and let herself fall onto the gravel. The color in her cheeks high, she slipped around the front of the truck, through the high beams of its headlights, and threw open the passenger door. She climbed in, plopping herself down, her one knee touching the black ball of the stick shift, while my father moved into the driver's seat and curled his fingers around the steering wheel. With the light off in my bedroom, I leaned against the opened window, watching them in the driveway and listening to the shrill, grinding sound of the gears as my father shifted into first. The truck jerked forward a foot or two, the brake lights flared red, and the engine clacked loudly before it stalled.

My mother said, "It's all right, Frank. It's been so long since you drove. You've just got to *ease* off the clutch, just *ease* off."

Then my father's reply: "It's supposed to be like riding a bike."

After that, my mother's loud laughter pealed out of the truck's open window.

The engine started again, my father eased off the clutch, and the truck rolled along the driveway to the right of the barn.

In the gathering darkness, my mother said, "Wait, wait, wait!"

I watched the truck screech to a stop before she slid out, hurried toward the pasture's split-rail fence, mostly fallen from disuse, and swung back the metal gate. They drove through, bouncing along in the cab as the tires hit gopher holes and dirt mounds. My father had an enormous grin on his face. My mother laughed as he circled the pasture, making figure eights then backing up and moving forward, for nearly an hour.

Afterward, my mother held his hand, and I watched her squat silhouette guide my father's lumbering frame to the picnic table in the backyard. She helped him sit, careful of his hip, then molded her body beside him. He slung his arm around her shoulder; she pressed her head against his chest. The moon rose low in the sky and washed the tops of their heads in a puddle of silver light. A few stars, like paint flicked from the bristles of a soft brush, dotted the black sky. My mother, curls falling away from her face, gestured above her head, swirling her finger and connecting the small pinpricks of light. She smiled, and my father, his hair grown thin and his jowls sagging, curled his arm tighter around her, pulling her mouth toward his. It was strange for me to see them like that, being loving, touching each other tenderly.

A thick knot lodged itself in my throat, and I grieved for things that were gone: Jolene as my confidant, my father as he was when I was small, my mother as the nurturer I needed. In my heart, though, as I watched my parents embrace, a small sprig of hope blossomed in my belly that maybe all wasn't lost, that maybe my family would be okay.

As it turned out, I was wrong.

April 1973

THE SECOND EXPLOSION came the month I turned eighteen.

Through the early morning fog, a fog so deep it drowned out the edges of the wide dirt road, the headlights of a Dodge Dart swung across a barbed-wire fence that sagged in a soft arc between the leaning fence posts lining an empty field. Thunder was rumbling far-off in the distance as the car skidded across the gravel, past a ditch filled with muddy water, and plowed into a telephone pole.

The driver's head and body plunged through the windshield. She shrieked into the otherwise silent morning, her voice mixing with busting glass and twisting metal as she pitched across the hood, shattering one arm and several ribs, puncturing a lung, and opening a wide, long gash in the flesh of her thigh. The leg wound sliced through an artery that pumped her blood in dark red spurts across the car's yellow paint. The telephone pole snapped her spine, and a nail head that kept some neighbor's scrawled bulletin fixed to the pole tore through her skin and held a clot of her body there. She spun into planted corn rows that hadn't yet sprouted and spattered blood and brain across the dirt. She tumbled to a stop, finally, as the slow rain beat down harder, and there, as the dirt churned into mud, she managed a few unconscious breaths and died.

While she was taking her last breaths a half-mile from our house, I sat at the kitchen table wearing frayed jeans and a blue sweater, my hair pulled back in a small ponytail. I hooked my bare heels on the bottom rung of the chair so my toenails, painted a bright, gaudy red, pointed at the linoleum. I sliced a circle from a log of summer sausage and nibbled on the edges. My mother in her robe and slippers, hair pinned back in a bun, moved from the kitchen counter to the refrigerator and back again. Her flurry of activity sent odors — honeydew melon, strawberry lotion, flour, and raw eggs — spinning through the air. Half her body bent into the refrigerator, she scoured the shelves, muttering, "Where is it? *Where* is it?"

"Where's what?" I said.

"The sour cream. Have you seen it?"

"Daddy finished it off yesterday with the potato chips."

She slammed the refrigerator, and the bottles inside the door clanked together. She stamped her foot and said, "Just how am I supposed to make muffins without sour cream?"

I shrugged. "Make them with butter."

She rolled her eyes dramatically then dismissed me with a few flaps of her hand. "Lord, you would think I spent all this time teaching you absolutely nothing. Sour cream makes it moist."

"Oh," I said.

I was still at the table and she had moved to the countertop, stirring butter into the batter, when we first heard the muted sound of the bullhorn in town calling the fire department volunteers. Shortly afterward, we heard the siren of Stanhope's one police cruiser getting louder, passing our house in a flurry of gravel and noise, and then fading again. My mother dropped the wooden spoon into the mixing bowl and stumbled into the living room, out the front door, and onto the porch. I slipped on a pair of sneakers and followed after her.

She said, "I wonder where Ned's going so fast."

Thunder cracked and rain pelted the ground when the fire truck came barreling down the road a few minutes later.

My mother said, "There must've been an accident." Then she caught a glimpse of my father in his soaked overalls, like a dark smear against the landscape, lumbering down the drive with a wrench in his fist. "Where's he going?"

She crossed the porch toward the gravel courtyard and wrapped her fingers tightly around the railing. The first hint of panic crept into her voice. "Jolene's car? Where's Jolie's car?"

The wind shifted and raindrops struck us, the cold and force of them stinging against my face and hands. I said, "By the barn."

My mother's quavering voice shouted, "No, it's not!"

Water dotted my cheeks, ran in streams along my hairline, and dampened my clothes so my sweater clung to my frame. A queasy feeling scuttled up from my stomach.

My mother rushed up to me and grabbed my wrist. Her eyes flicked across my face. "Where's your sister?"

I shrugged.

"Ann Marie!" She tightened her hold on me. "Have you seen Jolene this morning?"

I shook my head, saying, "No."

More to herself than to me, my mother said rapid-fire, "She's not allowed to drive on the road, just the pasture. She knows that. Besides, I didn't hear the car go out. With the muffler busted, you can hear that car a mile away."

I said, "Daddy fixed it."

Her babbling voice trailed off. A stunned look arranged itself on her face, her features stiff and rigid. "When?"

"A couple days ago."

My mother released me and bolted across the porch, sliding across the rain-slicked floorboards and through the front door, yelling, "Jolene! Jolene!"

My father paused at the end of the driveway. The rain came in sheets, soaking his clothes and matting his hair in clumps against his scalp. With the back of his sleeve, he brushed the water out of his eyes then bent his head against the wind. He hung a right as he passed the mailbox, shuffling along the shoulder of the road with the wrench still clutched in one hand.

I ran down the porch stairs and onto the grass. Rain pelted me like cold, sharp needles while thunder cracked overhead. Eyes on my father, I rushed across the soft, muddied lawn toward the driveway. I stopped at the mailbox to see emergency lights swooping blue and red in the distance, maybe half a mile away on the left, which made the accident scene O'Flannery's cornfield. A brief thought — *it might be Patrick O'Flannery and what would Jolie do if he got hurt?* — darted through my head.

I started to jog, the mud churning and splattering against the hem of my jeans. Somewhere up ahead, a woman's voice let out a high-pitched scream. A few yards in front of me, his back just an inky blot in the rain, my father crossed the road, dropped the wrench, and began a jerky, lurching run. I quickened my pace, catching up to him in a few long strides.

The volunteer firemen, most of them teenaged boys I knew from school, formed a loose perimeter. They stood with their hands dangling at their sides, shifting their weight from foot to foot and glancing from the ruined car in front of them to the shapes of my father and me as we drew closer. One of them yelled at the sheriff that Frank Adler was headed this way. Ned Horner, a chunky man with stubble lining his face, stood across the road with a twisted license plate gripped in one hand. He heard the shout and rushed forward, placing himself between my father and Jolene's mangled body.

"No man should remember his daughter like that," Ned said, his hand gripping my father's arm as we stood in the middle of the road.

Beyond Ned, one of the volunteer firefighters, a young boy maybe a year or so older than Jolene, doubled over and threw up near his feet. The sheriff guided my father away from the accident and toward the ambulance on the opposite side of the road. The kids I knew from school shored up their bodies one after the other, a human wall between us and Jolene, while rain soaked their faces and their clothes.

Bent at the waist so his head was near his knees, my father sat inside the back of the ambulance, clutching his hands against his skull and gasping for breath.

"Daddy?" I said, brushing my fingers against his shoulder.

At my touch, he glanced up at my face, his eyes searching. "Jolene?"

"No, Daddy, I'm Ann Marie."

"It's Jolene," he whispered. "I think Jolene's dead."

My heart thudded against my ribcage. My vision swooned and I fell backward, sitting down hard across from my father.

The sheriff leaned against the ambulance door, saying, "Take it easy. Take it easy."

Through the ambulance window, I saw Mr. O'Flannery, his lanky frame standing a good head above the young firefighters, red hair poking out from underneath his hood. His blue jeans and flannel jacket were stained with dirt, oil, and my sister's blood. He shook his head and frowned. He cracked his knuckles then glanced over at the ambulance, his green eyes staring at me. He spoke softly to the person beside him, and Mrs. O'Flannery, squat and dark in her black slicker, turned and met my gaze. I knew, as she walked toward the ambulance, that it was her scream I had heard.

"I got a right to see her," my father said suddenly, punctuating his sentence by pounding a fist against his thigh. "She's *my* daughter, *my* flesh and blood."

The sheriff hesitated then quietly said, "All right."

My father stumbled into the rain, crossing the road. I followed after him. Mrs. O'Flannery stopped us a few feet from the ambulance and said, "I'm so sorry." Mr. O'Flannery came up behind her and said in a calm, thin voice, "It's bad, Frank. Are you sure you want to see her like this?"

"She's my daughter," my father said again. His hands starting to shake, he added softly, "She's my little girl."

The firefighters parted, and standing at the edge of the ditch, we saw what remained of the yellow Dodge Dart my father had picked up not long ago at a salvage yard. My father stared at the fuzzy pink dice hanging cockeyed off the rear-view mirror, and the tremor in his hands moved along his arms until his entire body quaked. He followed the shards of the broken windshield across the hood, eyes lighting on the blood splattered down its length. He saw the telephone pole where it'd cracked from the impact and the sharp nail that held a piece of Jolie's cheek. He clenched his fists and gulped for air like a man choking. Beyond the pole, he saw a pile on the ground: bones and blood and skin. My sister's short hair fanned out across the dirt. Her clothes were dirty and torn. One eye stared forward while the other was just gone.

My father screamed. He punched his fist into the air. He kicked stones across the ditch, and they made tinny, tinkling sounds as they struck Jolene's twisted car. He yelled, "I ain't going to be no goddamned P-O-W!" He whirled around at the crowd of young kids milling about in their sneakers and jeans, torsos covered by dark-colored ponchos. "You won't take me that easy!" He ran down the middle of the road toward our house. He slipped a few times on the wet gravel before going down on one knee. The last thing I saw clearly before my head felt light and my joints buckled was Ned Horner rushing after him, a hand on his holster. Then I was falling, and a few firefighters seemed to cave in on me. I stared at their hazy faces, smooth and pliable as bread dough, and wondered as I struck the gravel road what it would be like to stick my fingers in that texture, to hold it and knead it and warm it with my palms.

Patrick's mother, her small, round face pink from the chill air, sat beside me in the ambulance, patting my thigh while I breathed oxygen through a mask. She said, "It's going to be all right, dear." A few minutes later, she was the first to spot my mother hurrying toward us alongside the road, clutching her mud-spattered robe about her waist, her fuzzy white house slippers matted and nearly black from the dirt and muck. I watched Mrs. O'Flannery mouth my mother's name. Her eyes flicked toward the sheriff, who stood near Jolene's car and spoke in low tones to Mr. O'Flannery. She leaned out the ambulance's back door and shouted, "Adele's coming!"

At the sound of her own name, my mother stopped some twenty feet up the road. Eyes darting, she saw her oldest daughter shivering in the back of an ambulance with an oxygen mask pressed to my face; her husband rocking back and forth in the back of a police cruiser, his fingers pressed against the window glass as he stared out at the field; her youngest daughter's small, crushed car beneath a telephone pole that was nearly snapped in half. Her face blanched. Her mouth opened in a wide oval before she clapped her palms against her lips, screaming into them over and over, "No! No! No! No! No!"

She bolted across the road, her hands flying into the air in front of her and her robe billowing open, exposing a thin, green nightgown molded against her thighs. One of her muddied slippers sailed off her foot and landed sideways on the gravel. I dropped the oxygen mask and rushed from the ambulance, yelling, "Mama! Mama, don't look!"

The sheriff, who had held Jolene as a baby, planted himself between my mother and Jolene. He grabbed her arms and forced her eyes to meet his. "Adele, you don't need the last image you have of her to be like that."

My mother glared at him and jerked her arm away. "If that's my daughter," she yelled, "then I need to see her!" She whipped her head around, meaning to see Jolene, but caught sight of Patrick's father in his bloodied clothes, and a small, shrill whine rolled out from the back of her throat.

Quietly, the sheriff said, "It's bad, Adele."

My mother wrapped her arms around her belly and moaned. She whispered, "Ned, I have to see her."

The sheriff helped my mother over the ditch, now flowing heavy with silt and rain. Tendrils of blood seeped along the ground, slid down the bank, and mixed with the black water already there. She stopped a foot or so away from Jolene and stared at the hollow cavity that had once held Jolene's right eye. She latched onto the sheriff's forearm, digging her fingers into his flesh.

He asked, "Adele, are you sure you want to do this?"

She stumbled toward Jolene's head, dropped to her knees, and pulled her dead daughter into her lap. Blood and brain trickled across the muddied terrycloth of her robe. She curled her nose into my sister's hair, breathing in the scent of Jolene that was still faintly there. As my father cried behind the glass window of the police car, as I stood numbly at the edge of the ditch and shivered in the cold, my mother started to rock back and forth, tears falling down her face, while she hummed a slow country tune.

She held Jolie that way for nearly half an hour, rocking her daughter against her belly, humming one tune after another. She didn't stop when the fire engine rumbled into O'Flannery's driveway, turned around, and headed back to town. She didn't stop when the first of the volunteer firemen shuffled back to his car and drove away or when Ned's voice cut through the air, telling the rest of them to go back home, the adults would handle things from here. She was humming still as ignitions turned over, mufflers rattled, and taillights disappeared over the gentle slope of the road near our house.

The rain softened into slow, easy drops. My mother watched the drops splash against the dirt of the cornfield. A gust of wind blew splinters of wood from the broken telephone pole into Jolene's matted hair, and still my mother hummed. Her knees sunk into the soft earth, and she curled her chin against Jolene's scalp, holding her dead child more tightly against her.

Finally, Ned Horner, who had been at the hospital nearly sixteen years ago for my sister's birth, was forced to say, "Adele, you have to let her go. It's time to take her to the morgue."

THE NEXT DAY at our house, the rooms drenched in a thick, heavy quiet, we all gathered in the kitchen, my father and I at the table, my mother next to the sink. His hands trembling, my father mentioned something about burying Jolene beside the baby under the apple tree.

"She needs a proper burial," my mother said, attacking an apple with a dulled peeler, ripping chunks of fruit that fell with soft, wet plops onto the countertop. "Someplace we can go visit." Softer, she added, "Someplace I don't have to see her every day. My heart couldn't take that."

"But what about David?" my father said.

"What about him?"

"Who's David?" I asked.

"The baby who died," my mother answered, glancing out the window above the sink at the yellow and brown finches fluttering in a rush of color and dullness around the birdfeeder. It occurred to me that up until then I had never known his name.

My father wandered outside, the day sunny and cool, and sat cross-legged in the shade of the apple tree. My brother's grave was just a mild rise in the land after all these years, a grass-covered bump that might've been mistaken for a root pushing through. The apple tree was bare-branched except for small feathery white buds that in a week or so would open into wide, pink blossoms. My father slouched beneath the boughs, peeling blades of crabgrass down the middle, squeezing them between his thumbs and against his lips, blowing as they whistled, staying outside all day until dusk reddened the sky.

"SHE'LL BE AT Evergreen Cemetery," my mother said to the bathroom mirror the morning of Jolene's burial. "She would've liked the colors in the fall."

I sat on the closed toilet lid, crossing my legs at the ankle, as she poked her tongue through her teeth and pressed a silver earring into her lobe. She smoothed strawberry-scented lotion on her face and down her neck then dabbed perfume behind each ear. As a young child, I had loved watching her dress, the makeup making her face look silky, the smell of Aquanet rolling off her stiff hair, the fold and curve of a dress sliding past her waist. It had been a long time since I'd sat beside her like that, and I noticed makeup caked in the small crevices around her eyes and lipstick feathered off her lips into the wrinkles around her mouth. I breathed in, smelling a tinge of sweet lilac perfume and the faint odor of ammonia from the dye she used to color her hair. I touched the hem of the black dress she'd pulled from the back of her closet and forced her body into, my father pulling the two sides together while I worked up the zipper.

My father was heavily medicated and stood at the edge of the bed, his eyes unfocused, his body stunted and thick, running a slow hand through his thinning hair. During normal days, he took a handful of pills to combat the schizophrenia, to reverse the side effects of other pills, to bring him up, to send him down. Since Jolene's death, he'd been on heavier dosages, leaving him wooden, leaden, lost. He was just outside the opened bathroom door, wearing dress pants loose around his hips and an untucked white button-down shirt, while he stepped forward and back again and again. Feet moving, he stared at the mattress, his fingers curling and uncurling. He stopped and blinked very slowly, holding his eyes shut for a long time before opening them again.

"Daddy, you all right?" I said from the bathroom.

He answered, "I need my belt. You seen my belt?"

"It's right there on the bed. The black thing wound in a coil."

"Oh," he said, his feet dancing forward. His fingers poised above it, he hesitated. "Looks like a snake. You sure?"

"I'm sure."

My mother gasped then grimaced, the constant fear that my father would once again not know us showing itself in her expression.

My father looked up, blank-faced, and tried to smile. "Little fuzzy," he said. "That's all."

My mother watched him dress and then wander from the room. She said, "I'll have to call the doctor again."

Behind her, I said, "I wish he didn't have to take all that medicine all the time. It makes him so tired. And he still won't talk to us ..." I paused, my tongue feeling thick in my mouth, my face flushing. "Me. He still won't talk to me. Not unless you're nearby."

She turned around, black-eyed from a lack of sleep. "Those drugs keep him from hurting you. They're all we have to keep you safe."

As I watched her stare into the mirror, mouth puckered as she dabbed on more pale pink lipstick, I wondered where she fell in the equation of keeping her children safe. I wondered if she knew about the guns to his head, the belts to our behinds, the chasings and the catchings, the haulings across the yard and the imprisonments in the cellar. And a memory plowed into me of Jolie writing a note asking for a hole punch, and the fulfillment of that request shining dully atop the box of supplies.

That thought led to another: *How did the box of supplies come to be down there at all?* As a child, Jolie used to keep small trinkets — blue feathers, red beads, yellow ribbon — in her pockets at all times, never knowing when my father would drag her to the cellar. But she never carried big items: reams of paper, bottles of glue, scissors, a propane lantern.

Softly, I said, "Why'd you leave that box down in the cellar for Jolene?"

The air in the room seemed to flatten as something big and unspoken came to share our space. My mother's hand shook and the lipstick fell, clattering into the sink basin, rolling to a stop against the drain. My mother smoothed her hands along the front of her dress. She whispered, "It was cruel to leave her down there all day with nothing to do."

"Why'd you let him leave her down there at all?"

She plucked the lipstick between two fingers and stuffed it in the plastic pouch that held her makeup. "I was trying to help her the only way I knew how."

"Why didn't you come and get her?"

My mother stamped her foot then glared at me. "Marie, can't we discuss this later? Your sister's being buried today."

"No," I said.

She huffed out a breath, turned on her heel, and stomped from the bathroom. Over her shoulder, she said, "I'm not going to talk about this now."

"Why didn't you come and get her?" I yelled.

My mother stopped near the edge of the bed. Her shoulders slumped as she sank onto the mattress. "I'm so tired. I don't have the energy anymore. I'm exhausted caring for him, making sure he takes his pills, keeping an eye on him all the time, shaving him, bathing him, making sure he doesn't eat this or that, not too much salt, just enough water to make sure the medicine works. You just don't know how hard it is. You just don't know. It was ... easier ... to let him put Jolene down there. Maybe it was the wrong thing to do, but it got so hard to confront him. Sometimes, he'd rage and throw things." Her voice softened. "Other times, he'd cry and threaten to hurt himself. I couldn't bear it. It was easier, Ann Marie, just to go along."

"You chose him over us," I said flatly.

"You judge me," she said, hunching over her lap, head bowed, fingers woven between her knees. "I didn't protect you. I sat in the house and watched. I'm as much a monster as your father, isn't that what you think? But you're not old enough, yet, to have impossible choices thrown at you. To choose this or that, knowing one will have to suffer."

I stood up, arms crossed in front of my chest, and leaned against the bathroom's doorjamb. "But it wasn't *you* that suffered, was it?"

She glanced at me, her bottom lip trembling, her eyes boring into mine so fiercely that I looked away. "I've watched the face of a man I've loved for as long as I can remember become unfamiliar to me. I've watched him struggle and rage and cry like a child, and I can't help him. There's nothing I can do. *Nothing.* The damage in his head is already done. There's no undoing it. All these medicines, they're just to *dull* his brain enough so that the delusions don't seem real to him anymore. Two of my children are dead. You are so unhappy. You don't think that's suffering for me?"

"I wouldn't have made my kids hate me," I whispered. "I would have left him."

She smoothed one hand across the comforter. "You say you hate me, but you would've hated me more if I'd taken you to live with Grandma Esther, if we'd had to live by the rules of her house."

"It would've been better—"

"No, Ann Marie, it wouldn't have. You can say things could've been this way or that way, but you can't ever know. Me, a housewife who got married right after high school and never worked anywhere but Bill's Diner, making lousy tips that weren't enough to eat breakfast on, let alone raise two kids. How could I leave him? There was nowhere to go."

"He put a gun to his head," I barked. "He said he'd kill himself unless I sang him a song. Did you know that?"

Her face paled. "I'm so sorry." Softer, "That was the war talking."

I roared up, my arms waving wildly in the air. "How can you keep defending him? How can you keep making excuses for him?"

"He's sick. I know you don't understand, but what's real and what isn't are all mixed up in his head. I loved him before the war. And after ..." Her voice trailed off, and a sad look crossed her face. "Well, after, there just weren't many choices." She stood up, her black dress swishing lightly against her legs. "We have to go to the wake now or we'll be late for our last chance to say good-bye."

MY SISTER'S SMILING face peered out from a brown frame above the lid of the closed coffin. It was her school picture, a picture she had hated. But it was the first one my mother had come across in the photo album, the first one she had clutched to her chest as she shook with a sadness so strong that it left her feeling cold and hollow.

At the funeral home, my family sat uncomfortably in the front row. A couple dozen people milled about, brushing up against us, offering us their condolences. My mother sat stiffly, her fingers kneading a white handkerchief in her lap. My father slouched in his chair, staring at the upturned palms of his hands and flinching whenever someone came near. I sat between my parents, glancing at Jolene's picture then at the purple-tipped lilies, red carnations, and dozens of yellow roses surrounding her coffin.

My mother dabbed at her eyes and whispered, "I wonder if it's dark there."

The black dress I wore chafed against my skin. My face felt hot and prickly as I said, "In the coffin?"

"No." My mother watched Patrick O'Flannery, red hair flaming against his dark blue suit, run his fingers along the coffin then let them hover above Jolene's face in the picture frame. "Wherever she is. Heaven, I guess."

Patrick's face crumpled and I said, "Heaven's supposed to be full of light."

"I used to sit in the dark when I was a girl," my mother whispered as Patrick kissed his fingers and ran them across Jolene's smiling face. "I used to sit there and wait for somebody to come rescue me."

"Jolie doesn't need rescuing anymore," I said as Mrs. O'Flannery placed her hand against the small of Patrick's back and steered him down the aisle to a red-cushioned seat near the back.

Quietly, we watched Ned Horner stand in front of Jolene's coffin, the sheriff's uniform gone and in its place a suit and tie, his face shaven, and the brim of a brown fedora held firmly to his chest. My mother said, "I'd sing small songs I'd made up. I was going to be a singer, you know? I'd sing words to keep their anger away from me, but their screaming arguments used to ooze through the floorboards and hang in the air like some kind of suffocating fog. I'd breathe all that hate right into my lungs."

Ned bowed his head and mouthed the words of a prayer. He wiped his eyes with the back of his sleeve, blinked a half-dozen times, then shuffled past our family, laying a quick, heavy hand on my father's shoulder. When he was gone, my mother said, "My mother would say to me, '*You're nothing great.*' She'd say, '*You won't amount to much of anything at all.*' "

After the line dwindled to no one, my father, slope-shouldered and overweight, lumbered the few feet to Jolene's coffin. He leaned his doughy face, the color nearly gray, close to the cherry wood and said in a low voice, "I'm sorry, Jolene. You deserved better than what you got. You deserved better than me."

My mother didn't seem to hear him. She stared straight ahead, her body stiff. "Maybe she was right about me. But Jolene was going to be an artist. Yes, she was. I never told her she couldn't. I was careful with what I said. I didn't want to discourage her. I didn't want her to grow up thinking her life was my fault. Not the way I did with my mother."

I thought, *Your actions spoke louder.* Out loud, I said, "Mama, it's our turn to say goodbye to Jolene."

My mother startled at the mention of Jolene. She glanced around at the room full of people, grabbed my arm, and said, "I can't. Not in front of all of them."

Twenty minutes later, everyone retreated into the cool sunlight outside except my father, who slouched in a high-backed stuffed chair near the doorway, and me, who sat in the front row. My mother inched up to the coffin, her body stooped as if she were ashamed. She laid a pale hand against the wood and sighed.

"Now two of my babies are in heaven." At first, her words came slowly then faster until they droned together like a florescent bulb's hum. "I didn't know it was hereditary and by the time I did, it was too late. You were born, and the damage was already done to your brain. The doctor said there would be no fixing it. I'm sorry I ignored the signs. The spasms and the tics. The jumping at things that weren't there. The doctor told me to watch, but I didn't want to see, Jolene. I didn't *want* to see."

My mother fell against the coffin, clutching the brass handle on the side. "I just ... I just ..." She paused, her body trembling as she barked out enormous, sucking sobs.

I curled my fingers around the edge of the chair, digging my nails into the cushion. I'd never known my sister had a sickness, something akin to my father's. I felt light-headed, like I couldn't get enough air to breathe. I closed my eyes, letting numbers fill my head, and counted until the rise and fall of my chest came easily.

When I opened my eyes again, my mother had sunk to her knees, weeping into her hands, begging through her tears. "I'd been through it with your father, the constant care, the constant monitoring. I wasn't strong enough to go through it again. I was so alone. Please forgive me, Jolene. I buried my head in the sand, trying to pretend it would go away."

In the waiting area, a blade of sunlight sliced through the window, and my father made small looping circles into the air with his index finger. There was so much I didn't know. My stomach felt shriveled, my gut a hard stone. My mother stood, scooped up the picture of Jolene, pressed it against her chest, and rushed up the aisle toward my father. Alone with my sister, the body in the coffin a horrific parody of what she had once been, I said softly, "Is it true, Jolene? Why didn't you tell me? Maybe I could've helped you."

IN THE LATE afternoon, we arrived at Evergreen Cemetery, a small plot of land with only a few dozen graves not quite a mile south of our house. Leaning against the wrought-iron arch entrance, their backs to the road, Ned Horner and Mr. O'Flannery spoke in low tones. As I helped my father from the station wagon, I heard the sheriff say, "County just dumped gravel. She should've known better than to be driving that fast on loose gravel."

"How fast?"

"Upwards of seventy miles an hour."

"Christ," Patrick's father said then spit on the ground.

"Telephone poles got to be at least a couple hundred feet apart," the sheriff said. "What're the chances of hitting one head-on like that instead of just winding up in the ditch?"

I stiffened, my grip tightening around my father's forearm, my gut lurching as they continued.

"What're you thinking, Ned?"

"Maybe it wasn't an accident."

"You know that for sure?"

"No way to know it for sure," the sheriff said. "Just a hunch. A bad feeling I got about the whole thing."

My father, his hearing failing, flinched at the pressure of my grip but not at any of the words coming from behind me. My mother, still in the driver's seat, dug through her purse, her attention focused on finding something. Loudly, I cleared my throat, and the men turned from the tombstones toward the road. The last words I heard were Mr. O'Flannery saying, "We'll talk about this later," and the sheriff's terse reply, "Yep."

Near my sister's gravesite, big-leafed ivy crawled along the trunk of an oak and choked the life from a scrub bush beneath it. Jolie's coffin hovered above a gaping rectangular hole, and dirt lay in a mound a few feet away, making her plot look ugly and harsh.

Wringing a small black purse between my hands, I watched my father limp toward the coffin, stop a few feet from it, and sway slightly back and forth. I wondered if he would remember any of this. All those drugs to keep him stable, and in the end, a year from now or a week or maybe even as soon as this afternoon, would he remember seeing her grave, would he remember saying goodbye?

I breathed a long, deep sigh. The little stone above my pubic bone pulsed. I didn't want to think about her being ill, about her death being a deliberate act. The preacher spoke a few soft words, and his voice reminded me of what it's like to be drunk — sort of numb and safe at the same time. I let myself fall into that voice, my thoughts all blending into a soft static as my father leaned stiffly on his cane, my mother cried, and sun drizzled through the clouds onto Jolene's coffin.

THAT NIGHT I dreamt of Grandma Esther.

We stood on the soft ground of the cemetery beside Jolene's grave with the sun blazing down and bringing out the blue tint of her hair. My grandmother wore the dark green dress she was buried in, and a big black purse swung near her hip.

"You're dead, Grandma," I said.

A sad smile crossed her face. She reached out and patted my hand. "It's true. It wasn't an accident."

"What?"

"Jolene killed herself."

In my dream, I staggered backward, tripped over an exposed tree root, and fell on my behind. "How can you know that? Is Jolie there with you?"

My grandmother knelt down easily, her arthritic knees fluid once again. "Jolene's not here where I am. But I watched her write a note to you before she died. I watched her stumble through a few rough drafts. I watched her pick through words. I watched her cry. She knew she was sick, you know? She knew she had what your father had."

I felt nauseated. There were so many questions, and I couldn't choose among them. I opened my mouth, but only a soft gurgling noise poured out.

"She didn't want to go," my grandmother said. "But she didn't want to live like your father." She paused then added, "She thought she could help."

"What?" I whispered.

My grandmother opened her purse, pulled out a white handkerchief, and dabbed at her face. "She did it to make things better."

"What're you talking about?"

"Go find her letter to you."

"Where is it?"

"In the cellar," she said, slipping the handkerchief back into her purse and fastening the clasp. "You'll know where to look."

I reached out to touch her wrinkled, age-spotted hand, and she disappeared. Gone until the next night and the next, returning for nearly a week until I worked up the courage to go down into the cellar.

THE CELLAR WAS dim, nearly dark, and my sister's sweet scent, peppermint and black licorice, lingered in the air. The air felt cool and moist against my skin as I switched on the flashlight I'd brought with me.

Drawings covered everything. Gouge marks sliced through the hard ground where Jolene had dragged the metal canning shelves away from the back wall and into the middle of the room. My sister seemed desperate for space. Last year, when I'd come down to the cellar on a whim, only two walls and part of a third had been decorated, and even on those there had been gaps between the pages, pockets of space where the dirt showed through.

I whipped the flashlight's beam wildly around the walls and was hard-pressed to find a blank place anywhere. Trying to find method from madness, I thought, *Maybe, the walls were a timer, counting down. Maybe, my sister decided that when not one more inch remained of open space, then not one more day remained of her life. Maybe, all these pictures were her last words.* But in my dream, my grandmother said Jolie had written a note, had cried over the words, and so I took a deep breath, gripped the flashlight tightly, and started to search.

I didn't see my father right away, squatting on an overturned crate beside one of the canning shelves, his eyes staring blankly at the east wall. It was only the thick, heavy feeling of not being alone, the way the hairs stood up on my nape, that made me turn slowly, shining the beam on his face.

"Daddy?" I said, and he stirred a bit. He cut his eyes from me to the stairs, and I knew, because for so many years Jolie and I had done it, that he was searching for an escape. I wanted so much to feel pleasure from that. I wanted to say, "How's it feel to be trapped and threatened and afraid?" But he was hunched and small on that crate. His face was sloped and dull now. His palsied hands shook from years of being medicated. Watching him, I realized that I was too late: The man I hated was gone, and the quaking person before me was all that was left.

"Mama's not coming," I said. "You'll have to talk to me."

First, he studied his upturned palms, then his booted feet. He didn't talk for a long time. I stood with the flashlight dangling from my hand, the beam a small oval against the dirt floor, and listened to him breathe. He drew in deep, rattling breaths and wheezed them back out. I was waiting, although I didn't know it right then, for the wick to burn down, for the third and final explosion to happen. I started counting the seconds — *one Mississippi, two Mississippi* — until he spoke.

At fifty-six Mississippi, he said, "She was talented. The pictures, they're all of me. I didn't know ..."

He paused. Afraid he wouldn't start again, I bleated, "Didn't know what?"

"I didn't know they were down here." He released his fist, and several small things slid between his fingers, falling to the dirt by his feet. "Is that how she saw me?" He glanced in my direction. "Is that how I was?"

When I was younger, I often thought about what it would feel like to press my thumbs against the soft flesh of his throat, to bump up against his windpipe and press down until his hands clutched at mine and his tongue, bluish and bloated, protruded from his mouth. I swallowed hard. The back of my throat burned. In the end, the only thing I could manage to do was nod. On the wall behind me, though, the pictures spoke quietly of him. They were filled with blackness — pitted eyes, clawed hands, and mouths full of sharp teeth.

"I didn't mean to be that way," my father said. "I'm sorry."

I took a few steps toward him, and looking down, I saw pills strewn about in the dirt near his feet.

"You should go," he said softly.

"Why didn't you take your pills?"

"I was too slow to help her."

I took another step forward, and this time, he flinched away from me. "Do you know who I am?" I asked.

It was a good while before he said, "Marie." He paused and pressed his palms in the hollows of his eyes. "For now, I know. When they finally wear off, maybe not."

I could feel the heat spilling off his body in warm waves. He was so close to being the father I needed. "I'll get you a glass of water and you'll take them and everything will be fine."

My father balled his fingers into fists and pounded them against his thighs in a move so sudden, so violent, that out of reflex, I backpedaled several steps. "She had a gift. I never knew that." He waved at the pictures on the wall. "She was my child, and I never knew that about her."

I sputtered, "It's not too late to know her."

"She's dead," he mumbled. "She's gone and these pills," he kicked the dirt where they'd fallen, "these pills left me too slow to help her."

"But I'm here. You could ask me. You could talk to me."

"Don't you understand?" he said. "In a few minutes, in a hour, maybe even a day, I won't know you."

"You know me now. Daddy, please. You know me now."

My father pointed high on the wall behind me. "Do you remember that toy gun?" Jolene had glued a gray plastic gun on a drawing of my father as a stick figure. The barrel pointed at the bulbous black stain that was his caricatured head. "You remember when you was seven years old and found it?"

"No," I lied.

"I followed you to the drainpipe out back because I was afraid you'd skin your knees playing on it. I was scared for you, and then out you came with this plastic gun. You pointed it at your head. 'Just like Daddy,' you kept saying, 'Just like Daddy,' over and over again."

I sunk to the floor, wrapped my arms around my shins, and rested my chin atop my knees. My head felt light, my vision unsteady. I breathed slowly, sucking wet-earth smelling air into my lungs.

"I remember," my father said. "I remember everything." After a little while, he added, "Wish I didn't."

"It was wedged under a log when I found it," I murmured.

"I never told your mother about it," he said, studying a mole on the back of his hand. "She kept after me all day. She said I looked shaken. Wasn't acting myself. My face was all sallow." My father snorted then looked over to me. "Sallow. Can you beat that? I didn't know what *sallow* meant. Still don't."

"Pale," I said softly, but he wasn't listening.

"Your mama likes to use those big words that don't anybody understand. She kept saying that word all day. Then she kept asking, 'Frank, what happened? Frank, what's the matter?' Dogging me all day until it occurred to me that your mama can be ruthless as one of them stray dogs stripping a bone, trying to suck the last tiny bit of meat off it." He grimaced and dropped his eyes back down to the ground. "I never did say though."

Light filtered down the stairwell and made a faint rectangle on the dirt floor. Sweat trickled between my breasts, soaking into the cotton of my bra. "Why not?"

My father pressed the hands that had once gripped me and dragged me across the lawn against his thighs to keep them from trembling. His dark hair, once shorn in a flattop, had grown longer and streaked with gray. He raised himself up, and the tall man who once towered over me now stooped in the dim light. He leaned heavily on his cane. "There was nothing I could say that would've made any kind of sense."

He lurched away from me. He limped toward the gun, reached up, and yanked it from the wall. He said, "Just like Daddy," before he shoved it deep into the front pocket of his overalls.

"Why didn't you tell Mama you were sick?"

Looking at the stairwell, he said, "They would've took me away. I already got took once. I got took to Korea, and that's what made me sick. I thought maybe if I stayed, you all would make me better."

"It didn't work out that way," I said.

"Naw. Didn't work out like I thought at all."

"Are you going to take your medicine?"

He glanced down at the dirt where the pills lay scattered. "They make me slow. Make me feel tired."

"You aren't a kind person without them."

His mouth pulled into a frown, and his chin started to quiver.

"Daddy, it's going to be all right."

He limped toward the stairs. Over his shoulder, he said, "Don't make much difference now."

The cane plunked onto the first step, and I said softly, "I'm still here."

He stopped. His back to me, he said, "My head don't work right sometimes. Wasn't the fault of you girls. Was my fault for not getting some help. Maybe you could forgive me someday?"

I wasn't ready to talk of forgiveness. My body still remembered: jerking away at sudden movements, nightmares that left me breathless and shaking, startling at unexpected noises no matter how small, a sheen of sweat that covered me whenever I met men for the first time. After the silence got thick between us, he continued up the stairs, his voice trailing behind him. "You clean off those pills, and I'll take them."

After my father left, I walked slowly near the walls, flashlight gleaming against a picture here or a poem there. I squatted in the corner near the stairs, touching my fingers first to the rut carved in the dirt then to the red paper where nearly a year ago I'd left my message for Jolene. In her tiny, backward-slanting script, she had written underneath:

Unless that seed falls to the ground and dies, it remains only a single seed, but if it dies, it produces many seeds. (John 12:24) That's the part I finally understand. Maybe things'll change now. I am that seed.

I backed away from those words. Out of my mouth came a low, strangled sound. My left temple started to pound.

I rushed over to the cardboard box of supplies and turned it upside down so paper, glue, scissors, and the like tumbled into a pile on the dirt. I had no particular thought in my head as I yanked the first picture from the wall, edges tearing and pushpins sailing through the air. Tears streamed down my face while I wadded it between my hands and slammed it into the box I'd just emptied. I tore down the next drawing and the next, chanting at first under my breath then later yelling over and over again, "No!"

What shocked me into stillness and silence was the map of my future self, the one I'd made all those years ago when Jolie and I had been in the cellar together. The paper was yellowed, the edges curled, but my future self was still there, a smiling woman in a light taffeta gown grasping the hand of a man in a dark satin waistcoat. And in the center, below a smattering of lopsided blue stars, was still Jolie's smooth, round seed, small as a sweet pea, the one she used to measure her faith. Breathing heavy, fingers bloodied from paper cuts, I plucked that seed with my thumb and index finger then shoved it deep in the pocket of my jeans. With a loud wail, I started to rip again, fingers hauling down every last drawing until sweat dripped from my hairline, a crazed pattern of tread marks littered the floor, and the walls were bare.

I hefted the box against my belly to carry it from the cellar, and as I stepped from the last stair, I stared up at the bluish sky. Geese flew overhead, traveling back north after the winter. I walked across the lawn toward the barn, my feet rustling a few dead leaves snagged on the grass. I knocked the box against the rim of a rust-eaten 55-gallon drum just outside the barn, and Jolie's drawings tumbled into it. I ripped the supply box down its seams, flattened it, and smashed it down into the soot-filled container. Near my father's workbench inside the barn, I found lighter fluid and a box of matches.

The cardboard burned slowly, flaring yellow and orange then charring black. Standing beside the drum, heat pouring from the top and warming my skin, I thought of my future self, the photograph of my face small as a postage stamp, burning, melting, crumbling into nothing. One side of the box turned to ash and caved in on itself. Sparks and bits of paper scattered. I found a long stick and jabbed at the fire to make sure everything burned. The wind changed and smoke filled my eyes, but still I kept stirring. When the sun had moved low on the horizon and the fire was just embers, I turned and went back to the house.

From the edge of the living room, I watched my mother on the couch, her fingers, stiff with the beginnings of arthritis, woven through an afghan she was knitting. She hummed and tapped her foot. She purled a row, sometimes two, then stopped humming, dropped the needles in her lap, and rubbed her knuckles. Slouched on the sofa, head dipping toward her chest and elbows pressed tight against her body, she seemed somehow diminished. Some ten minutes after I came into the room, she tilted her head toward me, breathed deeply through her nose, and said, "Smells like smoke."

"I burned some things from the cellar."

Her hands stilled. "Jolene's things?"

I nodded.

"Why?"

"They were old. Not good for anything anymore."

"They were memories."

I stared over my mother's shoulder, out the window, catching sight of the buckeye tree, bare-branched yet, its trunk almost black. "They weren't good ones, Mama. I don't think you would have wanted them."

At my mother's feet lay a shoebox filled with old photographs. She shoved the afghan aside, pulled the box to her lap, and rummaged through the pictures. As she searched, she said, "The man he was ... he was such a sweet, gentle man. I wish you could remember him like I do. We would go to the lake and crumble bread for the birds to eat. He would cry on the Fourth of July while the national anthem played."

She held a picture the size of a postcard into the air between us, and I crossed the room and sat down beside her. It was a colorless photograph of me in a bathing suit, standing on a beach while the surf brushed against my ankles. My father crouched next to me holding a plastic pail and shovel. I flipped it over, and in my mother's wobbly scrawl was, *Marie, 4, Bar Harbor.*

"Why are you showing me this?" I said.

"I wanted you to see the man he was."

"Why?"

She smiled sadly. "I've made so many mistakes, Ann Marie. So has your father. You'll leave soon. You'll meet a boy and get married. Forgive us or not. Have a life free of bitterness and hate or not. I can't make that choice for you. All the mistakes we made, we can't undo."

I let the photograph flutter out of my grasp and onto the floor. "You never protected me."

My mother plucked the picture from the carpet and set it atop all the others in the shoebox on her lap. "No, not the way you needed to be. This is all I have to offer now. This bit of advice that might save what's left for you."

It might have been anger, it might have been spite, although mostly I believe I just wanted someone to share in my utter grief, to comfort an ache so big it was overwhelming, that made me say, "She killed herself."

My mother's grip loosened, the shoebox fell, and photographs fanned out across the floor. She whispered, "What?"

Flatly, I said, "It wasn't an accident."

She blinked a few times. Her body started to shake, small tremors in her hands, moving up her arms. She grabbed at the fabric of her pants, crushing the material against her palms. She ran her tongue across her lips and said, "That's not true. You just want to hurt me."

My mother scooted off the couch and waded through photographs of a time when the memories weren't painful. Without looking at me, she said softly, "We did the best we could. It's not easy being a parent. Someday, you'll see. Someday, you'll understand the choices I made."

THE NEXT MORNING in a soft rain, I walked past the crash site where people had propped flowers and candles in the dirt. Someone had made a cross from two white birch twigs and planted it in the dark patch on the ground where Jolie's body had finally come to a stop. Something crackled in the air where my sister had died, something electric that I felt plugged into, so I stepped across the ditch and put the flat of my hand against the wood of the telephone pole. It had been cleaned, the neighbor's bulletin taken down, my sister's flesh removed. A sliver of wood cut my thumb, and I stuck it in my mouth, sucking at the bubble of blood welling up. A memory flooded into me of a picnic table that had sliced into my palm at Vacation Bible School when I was nine and Jolie seven. That memory pinned me like a spear to the spot on the ground, the dirt still scattered and darkened by her blood, where Jolene had died.

At the camp, I had run my palm along the edge of the table, feeling the warm groove of the wood. As a sliver lodged itself into my skin, a counselor read, "*I tell you the truth, unless a kernel of wheat falls to the ground and dies, it remains only a single seed. But if it dies, it produces many seeds.*"

Jolie, gap-toothed and in pigtails, leaned her small head closer to mine and whispered, "Do they mean you're not good to anybody unless you're dead?"

"I don't think so," I said, pressing a fingernail into my palm.

"Well, what then?"

"Dying to yourself, I guess. Not doing what you want."

"And if you do what you don't want? That'll change things?"

"I guess so."

Later that summer, as we were walking past O'Flannery's cornfield, the stalks bending in the wind, she said, "I'll be like that someday."

"What do you mean?"

But she just grinned back at me and never did give an answer.

Raindrops splattered across my face. At my feet, the first green shoots of corn sprouted through the dirt. Closer to the ditch, a small plant bloomed tiny purple flowers. A wicked taste scuttled into my mouth, and I stumbled away from the telephone pole, not yet ready for life to shuffle along. I jumped the ditch and spit that thick taste onto the road before I headed back home.

At the end of the driveway, my mother pulled the lid off a garbage can and threw something inside. As I got closer, I could see it was the map of Vietnam that my father had taped to a corkboard and hung on the basement wall. With black pushpins, he had marked American casualties near places with names you couldn't even pronounce. *Ia Drang. Khe Sanh. Tan Son Nhut.* He had said, "All them boys dead. Christ, don't it ever stop?" In the rain, my mother took the whole thing and dumped it in the trash.

"You should save the corkboard," I said. "It's a good piece of corkboard."

"I don't want any memories," my mother answered. "I have enough memories."

"Did you tell Daddy?"

"No. He's got enough memories, too."

JOLIE'S DEATH WASN'T mentioned again. My father swallowed pills and remained in a stunted state. Sometimes he spoke to me, other times not. My mother started taking pills, too. Pills to help her sleep. Pills to help her stay awake. Pills that left her slow and numb. I steeped in my grief, clawing at someone to help me, my fingers not finding purchase in the people closest to me, and so I decided to leave Stanhope, to leave Ohio, a few weeks later.

The morning I left, just as the sun started to rise, I slid out the front door and noticed small green apples forming on the apple tree in the front yard. Birds fluttered across the lawn. The southern side of the buckeye tree bloomed cones of white flowers. I dumped a duffle bag of my belongings into the old brown Impala my parents had picked up at a junkyard a year ago and rumbled down the driveway, taking a right onto the dirt road, dust kicking up under the tires. Less than a minute later, I passed Patrick O'Flannery squatting on his haunches at the edge of the cornfield where Jolene died. I pulled onto the shoulder, got out of the car, and crossed the road.

"I loved her," he said, his eyes red-rimmed from crying. "I would've asked her to marry me."

I shoved my hands deep in my pockets, staring at him past the ditch that separated us. "She would've said yes."

"Why'd she have to die?"

"I don't know."

In his hand, he crumbled the dirt that had held her body. He let it sift through his fingers as he said, "What do I do now?"

"I don't know that either, Patrick."

"What're you going to do?"

"I'm going away. Somewhere not here. Somewhere not Ohio."

"Will that fix it?"

In the pocket of my jacket, my fingers slid across Jolene's seed, the one I had plucked from the cellar. "Maybe."

He pinched a corn sprout between his long fingers and yanked it from the ground. He stood up, his jeans muddied, his thin shoulders caved inward, and faced me. "If you pull up the roots, they die." He thrust the sprout toward me, roots dangling loosely in the breeze. "Sometimes that happens to people."

"They die?" I said.

"If they pull up their roots."

We were quiet for a time. Birds chittered. Gravel crunched under my feet. Off in the distance, a train whistled. He let the sprout fall back down to the ground then said, "Will you come back?"

"No," I said quietly. "I don't think so."

June 1999

OVER THE LAST two and a half decades, I had spoken to my parents on the telephone only, maybe, a dozen times. I'd sent cards at Christmas with my name signed at the bottom. Sometimes I'd even sent letters. My mother had asked to see me a few times, and I'd said I was busy, I wasn't ready, it wasn't convenient, then eventually just simply, no. She mailed me pictures once, my father looking frail in the sunlight while she squinted at the lens. In the letter that accompanied the photographs, her cursive wobbled, the quaking of her hand leaving blots of black ink like paint spatter across the page. She asked me if I wouldn't please come home, just once, my father wasn't well.

Shortly after that letter, over twenty years ago now, in the grocery store near my house, I thought I saw her. I was partway down the canned-goods aisle, reading labels, trying to find sweet yams when my toddler son, nearly three years old, yanked several cans of kidney beans from the shelf and spun them across the floor. My newborn daughter was sleeping in the cart as I swooped down to collect the cans then caught a woman out of the corner of my eye — the light swish of her hair, the curve of her jawline — as she turned and vanished around a cardboard sign. I scurried to the end of the aisle, cans clutched to my belly, and stared into the face of a young woman dressed in black then past her at a display of oranges arranged like a pyramid. My mother, if it had been her, was gone. I remembered thinking, my heart pounding in my chest, my hands shaking as I restacked the fallen cans, *I'm not ready to see her. Not yet. Besides, it couldn't have been her. I live in Montana now. She wouldn't have driven all this way.*

After cancer had eaten a hole in my low belly, the doctor scooping out my ovaries and then my uterus, I had needed to understand why, so I finally went home. Now, it was me who was driving, moving east on the interstate, passing semi-trucks and a few cars, headlights blinding in the darkness as the hour got late, later. My ears filled with a seashell roar, as they always did when fear simmered in my belly. I drove all night, and in the morning, the space between my shoulder blades began to ache then my left temple to throb. As I crossed the Ohio state line, I started to count, numbers filling up my head to comfort me. By the time I arrived in the town where I'd grown up, I had already reached into the thousands and it was mid-morning, the sun riding low in the sky.

I passed over a set of railroad tracks that sliced through the hard ground and drove past a green sign — STANHOPE, pop. 1,500 — just beyond them. A weight seemed to settle on my chest, the memory of myself as a teenager in the backseat of a car, filling the air with quick, nervous laughs at the edge of the railroad tracks after the fog swept in. I kept driving, past farmland that rambled on for miles, past the street (paved now) where I would find my childhood home, and for another mile until the speed limit slowed to twenty-five and the two-lane road opened into the town's square. The hardware was still there on the corner, the windows filled with hand-written signs advertising tools, tractor parts, a brush-hog at half-price. I passed the one-room movie theater, boards over its doors and windows, the ticket booth outside dark and dusty. I eased around the square, staring out the passenger's window at the bank, the lone gas station, the grocery store, a few new shops I didn't recognize (a carpet place, a Radio Shack, a video store simply called The Den), the Goodwill, and finally Bill's Diner with a small sign tucked in the front window, Under New Management.

I drove halfway around the square again, turning down the outlet leading east, and reached the man-made lake that was the border of Stanhope. It was also the place where my family would go during the summers — my mother grilling hot dogs near the water's edge, my father swimming, my sister and I sunning ourselves on the grass — before my father's illness became an overwhelming thing. Two small children and their mother walked beside the shore, the woman smiling, squatting down, and pointing toward a handful of ducks bobbing along on the water. I moved on, driving across the causeway that split the lake in two. At the end of it, I slipped off the road into the gravel parking lot of the American Legion, where my father, when I was very small, used to spend Saturday nights slinging back beers, slapping his palm to his thigh, and serving up long, winding tales about Korea. I doubled-back, took a left at a McDonald's that used to be a pizza place, and there, tucked way in the back behind some pine trees, was the Stanhope Church of Christ.

My wet, muddied minivan idled in the empty parking lot for a long while, exhaust spilling into the cool air. There was such a sadness, sifting through the air like dust and powdering everything I saw. I was forty-four years old, dark lipstick feathering in the crevices of my chapped lips, wearing horn-rims now, my face round, my black hair shorter and pulled back. I was slope-shouldered, pudgier. Married and divorced. Not the same person as twenty-six years ago. Not the same person who slipped out one crisp morning and, without so much as a goodbye, hadn't ever come back. I angled my gaze, staring up at the steeple and the wide sky beyond it, waiting for the roar in my head to quiet. When it eventually did, I set my jaw, took a deep breath, and decided it was time to finally go home.

Minutes later, as sunlight drizzled faintly through the heavy clouds, I stopped at the bottom of the long gravel driveway, right beside the mailbox with its faded, red flag raised. The narrow driveway dipped across the land for a quarter of a mile before it emptied into a wide, round courtyard. To the right, the two-storied, whitewashed house sat stark against the concrete-colored sky. The roof of the front porch sagged to one side, its wood softened and rotted. Above that, the four-paned window of what had once been my little sister's bedroom seemed naked without curtains, the glass grimy with dust. From that window, you could look across the front lawn to the giant buckeye tree, six-stories tall, cones of flowers blooming on it now, its trunk black. Down a gentle slope south of the tree, the large pond, green algae skimming its surface, still sat in a depression in the land. To the left of the gravel courtyard, the grain silo had caved in on one side, the rusted tin cap pointing like an arrow toward the barn. The wood boards of the barn's sides were weathered now, some chipped, others broken or missing entirely. Husks of a few empty birds' nests — bits of hay, some small pieces of red fabric, the torn edges of a newspaper — dotted the crumbling eaves. Surrounding the barn, yellow wildflowers studded the pasture with blooms where once, a very long time ago, a few horses and a handful of cows had grazed. The split-rail fence that marked it was mostly fallen down, fence posts leaning in the soft mud, rails scattered and haphazard with disuse. Beyond the fence lay the remainder of my father's three hundred and fifty-three acres — pockmarked land, barren except for a few scattered stalk nubs where once there had been wheat, corn, and hay. The house faced west toward the road, and to the north, all along the length of the driveway, the pine trees planted years ago to act as a windbreak still creaked in the breeze. At the front edge of the gravel courtyard, a few feet from the driveway, grew that single apple tree, its branches thick with leaves and the round nubs of young fruit.

All these years later, my mother knelt in the dirt of a garden planted beside the house. She glanced up at the sound of the car's engine, cocked her head a notch, and stared across the courtyard, down the driveway, toward me. She stood up, shimmying a few steps across the lawn, stiff-legged from the arthritis that swelled her joints. She raised her right hand to her forehead for shade. At the end of the driveway, I rolled down the window. The wind carried the faintest tinge of her strawberry-scented lotion, of car grease from the barn, and, I swear, of my younger sister's favorite candies, peppermint and black licorice.

I clutched the steering wheel, pressed my forehead against it, and breathed soft, sucking gasps while tears fell and stained my lap. Sitting there, remembering, I fully understood the inklings of my own disease started all those years ago when my father first lost his mind. It was then that I started plugging all my rage, anger, and frustration into a small knot in my gut, the tissues bruising easily, softening and then rotting. Over the years, I had kept doing it, tucking away every unsaid want, unmet need, lost hope, and unfulfilled dream in that little place just above my pubic bone, and the cancer festered, spreading slowly, consuming my cells like rust does metal until one day there was nothing left to salvage from something that had once been beautiful and whole.

Twenty-six years ago, I'd driven west with no thought in my mind except to leave Ohio, hoping to go fast enough and far enough that the things haunting me wouldn't be able to keep up. In Butte, Montana, I had understood there was a hole inside of me from Jolene's death, and I was scrambling to fill it. I also understood that no matter how far I ran, it would still be there. Some mornings, I woke up with the sun on my face and I would curl myself into a ball and cry for Jolene, for the older brother I never knew, for the mother and father I wanted and never got. I cried until my lungs ached, my cheeks hurt, and a sharp pain started to pulse in my low belly, crimping my gut just above my pubic bone. I started to go to church when no one was there and sat in a pew, staring at the ceiling and begging God, if He was really there, to make it all stop.

Life went on like that for nearly a year. I waitressed at a little place called The Iron Skillet, and that's where I met Sam Jackson, a tall, bulky man of twenty-one, who left me nice tips, then wild flowers, and finally a ring. At age nineteen, I said yes. A year later, I gave birth to a boy, Sam Jr., and nearly three years after him, a daughter, Kathleen.

What I never realized until I lay night after night beside a man, his chest rising and falling, a light snore slipping past his lips, was that I was terrified of the things that might go wrong with his mind. Fear that a man would hurt himself and it would be my fault had lodged itself in me like a cocklebur all those years ago. That fear eventually spilled over onto my husband, so when it came time to be intimate — to confide secrets, to make love — I often backpedaled, making excuses and busying myself, until one day, at age twenty-four, I came home and Sam was just gone, leaving only a simple note at the table where he should've been.

That night, after the children were in bed, I stood in the shower and screamed while hot water rained into my mouth. I swallowed, beat my fist against the tiled wall, and screamed again. When my voice went hoarse, I slid down the wall until I knelt on the bathtub's floor, remembering the words I'd written as a child about my future life, saying over and over, "A man who loves me. A man who loves me." A few weeks later, the papers arrived in the mail, and not quite five years after we'd married, Sam and I quietly divorced.

I worked as a waitress for a few years. I learned to type and became a secretary. I bought a small house and raised my children. On and off through the years, I thought about going home. I would recall my father's illness, the gun pressed against his forehead while he said, *Sing me a song, angel, or I'll pull the trigger*. I thought of my mother, her words always echoing in my head, *Please don't ask me to choose, Ann Marie. I'd have to choose him*. I would remember my sister's short hair fanned out across the dirt, her clothes dirty and torn, one eye staring forward while the other was just gone. My gut would clamp down, and I knew I'd find no refuge in Stanhope, Ohio. Eventually, I was gone so long, I just didn't know how to begin to go back.

The year I turned forty-three, the doctor found the malignant lumps, and I went to church and got baptized. I met with the minister for two months afterward, asking questions about healing and faith, before he leaned forward in his chair, leveled his eyes at me, and said, "Look, Ann Marie, you won't ever be healed until you face what's tying you up in knots. You have to forgive your parents for being what they were. And you have to forgive Jolene for dying."

I had held onto all that rage like a bad debt, stuffing it into my belly, demanding a payment from my family that would never be forthcoming. As I sat in the minivan at the end of my parents' driveway, sobs shaking my body, it occurred to me that I could never go back and make my childhood something that it wasn't. I finally understood that for all these years I'd been trying.

I was crying still when my mother touched my sleeve. I lifted my head from the steering wheel and saw her age-spotted skin. Arthritis had curled her fingers into the palm of her hand, the knuckles immovable. I followed the line of her arm, across her pale neck, and saw her right eye was milky with a cataract. Her once-silky skin hung in folds along her jawbone. Wrinkles framed her mouth. Her hair, dark-colored the day I left, was completely gray. Time had curved her spine, a small hump jutting underneath the brown, button-down sweater she wore. Her body was all angles now. The curve of her clavicle used to be soft with flesh, a cushion when she held me, but now her skin was thinner, the bone sharper. She held a trowel in her other hand, and dirt sifted off its tip onto the ground.

"Ann Marie," she said.

In gasps that cut off my words, I said, "The sadness ... that was here, Mama ... and the rage. It's a wonder ... it didn't blow ... this house apart."

"It blew our family apart instead," she murmured, moving her crippled hand to cup mine.

I glanced toward the house and thought of my bedroom closet, the slashes it held where a knife marked my remaining days. I'd kept the tally in my head for all these years: 2,131 cuts in the wood, tiny notches in the wall, the last slash made on the morning I left, twenty-six years ago.

Outside the car door, my mother also stared toward the house, but her gaze lighted on the small garden beside it. Softly, she said, "I used to think heaven must be like gardening. There was a time when my hands were strong and straight, and I could plunge my fingers in the rich earth. I'd raise handfuls of dirt to my face and think heaven must be something like this. Heaven would be squatting among my plants and speaking softly to the sprouts, trying to help them to grow."

She patted my hand, and when I looked at her, she said, "Maybe things would've turned out better if I would've done that for you kids. Spoke to you softly, I mean, and tried to help you grow. In the dirt, I was fearless and strong. My life was perfect. There was no war to change my husband or breaths my son didn't take or the begging voices of you and Jolene. There was just the smooth landscape that my life should've been."

My mother climbed in the passenger's seat, and I drove slowly up the narrow driveway. We didn't speak for its quarter-mile length, and when it emptied into the wide, round courtyard, my mother said, "Lord, I've made so many mistakes."

She got out of the car and moved over to her garden, dropping the trowel into the tilled rows. In the car, I stared at the whitewashed house, at the window of my bedroom that held my mother's sewing mannequin and a bolt of blue fabric. Purple tulips bloomed in a row alongside the side door. The moonvine on the trellis had unfurled its wide, green leaves. With one foot in the foyer, my mother motioned for me to come inside the house. After I slid out of the car, she said, "I'll make some coffee. You go in the bedroom and see your daddy. He'll be so happy you're here."

My father sat in a wheelchair near the window, the slatted blinds filtering light in faded bars across his blank face. His skin was pulled taut over his bones. His body slumped to one side, and saliva leaked from his mouth and stained his blue sweatshirt. His hair was nearly gone, and underneath, his pate was speckled with age spots. His right arm, held close to his body, shook. His hands were frail and crooked. Tufts of a plastic diaper poked out from the waistband of his gray sweat pants.

"Daddy?"

His neck swiveled toward the sound. He caught sight of me and picked a quaking hand from his lap, patting the armrest of his wheelchair.

"Daddy?" I said again.

"Adele, that you?"

"No, it's Ann Marie."

"It's cold in here, ain't it?"

I found a blanket in the closet and tucked it around him. Standing beside him, I stared out the window, watching what he watched — cardinals lingering on the feeder, the propane tank rusting on the lawn, a groundhog scampering into a hole.

My father tugged at the hem of my white blouse, waited until I looked down at him, and said, "Is Adele serving peas tonight?"

"I don't know, Daddy."

"Because I ain't never liked peas."

My throat tightened. I whispered, "You used to sit in the garden and eat them off the vine. Mama used to get mad because the peas never made it into the house to get cooked."

He cocked his head a notch. "Who'd you say you was again?"

"I'm Ann Marie, Daddy."

He stared at me for nearly a minute before he said, "Ain't we related?" My father huffed onto the glass, fogging the pane, and his dentures slipped so they sat crooked in his mouth. "Aw, horseshit. I just can't remember." He held a finger to his lips and said, "Shhh. You hear that? Somebody's calling for help."

I heard my mother clinking coffee cups in the kitchen and several birds chittering outside. I said, "I don't hear anyone."

My father raised a shaking hand and wiped at the window. Peering out, he said, "Edgecomb bit it, didn't he?"

"Who?"

"He was calling for help. His mouth kept moving even after he got shot in the throat. Ain't no sound come out after that, though."

I knelt down, curling my fingers around his knee. "Are you talking about Korea?"

My father leaned toward me, his face so close to mine, I could smell the sourness of his breath. His eyes were hard and mad. "I saw them coming, you know? In from behind the trees, coming at us. I was scared. My mouth didn't work. I tried to yell something, but nothing came out of my mouth."

"That happened a long time ago."

He grunted. He stared out the window again, watching the sun burn the dew from the grass. After a while, he said, "Has the mail come?"

I moved over to his bed and sat on the edge of the mattress. I stared at him, this man who had made me fear all these years, and with a sharp twinge in my belly, I realized I wasn't much more than a stranger to him. "No, I don't think so."

"Check that drawer by the bed. She's always hiding my mail in the drawer."

I found, inside the nightstand, a bundle with some newspaper clippings, a dozen letters scratched out on notebook paper, a handful of Christmas cards with their creases nearly worn through from being folded and unfolded, and a slew of pictures stained by coffee, food, and the oils from my father's skin. I undid the rubber band and pulled off a letter from the top. It was dog-eared and torn, stained red near the bottom, the writing faded, but still I recognized my own slanted printing.

I remembered hunching over the desk in my basement, a small lamp spilling light in a circle, the seat of the wood chair worn in the shape of my rump. I remembered writing and scratching out, crumpling the paper and starting another. I had been torn between politeness on the page and bitterness in my heart. I must've composed a dozen drafts; in the end, I gave up and wrote a few lines that didn't mean much to me. But sitting on that bed as the morning sun threw shadows across my face, I saw how much they had meant to my father.

> *Hello Mama,*
> *I have two babies now. I think I told you about Sam. He'll be three in a few months. Kathleen came on December 3. I hope you and Daddy have a Merry Christmas. Tell him that I hope he gets better soon.*
> *Love, Ann Marie*

Underneath the letter was a creased photograph of my kids and me in that grocery store from twenty-some-odd years ago. I hadn't seen the camera. I hadn't really seen my mother, except for a swish of hair and the curve of a jawline. In the picture, my toddler son stared at the camera, my infant daughter slept in the cart, and my face tilted down as I reached for the cans of kidney beans that had fallen.

My hands shook as I laid that picture atop the comforter. There were other pictures in the stack: my little brown house, my son in the yard with an enormous grin on his face, me hanging wash on the clothesline, the German Shepherd scampering across the lawn. I shuffled through the images, mouth agape, not sure how to feel about my mother documenting my small life all those years ago without my knowing it as I stared into the sky with a clothespin in my hand. There were dozens of yellowed clippings from Butte's local newspaper: my wedding announcement, the birth of first my son and then my daughter, a small blurb when the divorce was granted, pictures of my daughter playing volleyball, pictures of my son when he won the state championship in chess. My father's big fingerprints smudged them all. There were places where he'd dog-eared the corners, where he'd left saliva and juice stains.

My father wheeled over to where I sat. He picked up my wedding announcement, my young face smiling brightly, and crinkled it when he pressed it tightly against his chest, just above his heart. He said, "I know you. You're that little girl who used to dance around on top of my boots. The one who wore a little nightgown that twirled up so high your underwear showed."

My hands fell limply into my lap, scattering letters and pictures across the mattress. My father smiled up at me, his teeth crooked. I said, "Yes, I'm that little girl."

"You're bigger now."

"A little."

"There was another little girl there with you. She used to jump up and down saying, 'Me too, Me too.' "

"Jolene," I said.

"That's a pretty name."

He set the announcement on the bed, reached into the nightstand drawer, and pulled out a sheet of paper. On it were numbers and words written in crayon. He smoothed it on his lap and read, "If I had to do it all again. One, be a better husband. Two, be a better father. Three, say no when the Army comes." He glanced up and grinned then shoved the paper into my hands.

"No, Daddy, this is yours."

"It was for you," he said. "I wrote it for you." His top dentures slipped further, and he took them out, plunking them into a glass on the nightstand where they drifted through the water and clinked faintly against the bottom.

My mother knocked on the opened bedroom door. "Coffee's ready."

My father's head turned to track her voice, and his eyes dulled, the lucidity scurrying back to wherever it had been hiding inside him.

"No, wait. Please," I begged.

"Did you bring tapioca?" my father asked her.

"No, Frank. We'll be having coffee," my mother answered.

"Daddy?" I clutched at his arm. "It's not too late."

He turned and held my face between his warm palms. "Please tell Bobby I'm sorry. I shouldn't've done that. I see that now."

"Who?"

"Edgecomb."

"No, Daddy. Please," I said, but he wheeled away from me toward the kitchen.

My mother stepped back to let him pass then walked over to the bed, lowering herself onto the mattress, facing me with bits of my life spread on the comforter between us.

"You took these," I said.

She nodded. "I wanted to make sure you had a happy life. You're the only baby I have left."

I skimmed my finger across the pictures, picking one from the bedspread. "He doesn't remember me."

"He will," she said. "Just give him some time."

I stared at the black and white photograph in my hand, the same one my mother had shown me in the days before I left. I turned it over to see her wobbly scrawl — *Marie, 4, Bar Harbor* — then flipped it back. "I had cancer," I said softly to the young me on the beach. "All these years I've held a grudge in my belly, eating away at my insides, and it's not even the faintest flicker of a memory to him."

My mother laid a hand to my knee. "I asked God to forgive us, Ann Marie. Maybe you can, too."

And at the mention of God, Jolie's Bible verse, once pinned to the cellar wall, flooded into me in bits and pieces.

Love is patient, love is kind. I thought of all the things that were supposed to be good in my life — my childhood, my relationship with my parents, my marriage, my bond with my own children — that had turned out badly.

Love is not self-seeking. I saw Jolene in the shadow of my mother's aged face. I thought of my German Shepherd that got hit by a car some fifteen years ago, his shattered body in a heap on the street, and how I held him against my knees as the life bled out of him. There on the asphalt, stones digging into my knees, I had wept for all the people who were gone from my life, wailing their names — Jolene, my parents, my ex-husband — into his matted fur.

Love keeps no record of wrongs. I thought of all the time that was gone now. The wedding my mother didn't get to see. The divorce she couldn't comfort me through. The grandchildren she'd never hold as babies because they were adults now. All the time I spent enraged and unforgiving. All the years I felt small and unimportant. *It's over*, I told myself. *No more.*

It always protects, always trusts, always hopes, always perseveres. Love never fails. I gathered up the pieces of my life — the pictures, papers, clippings — and dropped them in the drawer. Near the bottom of the pile, in a small depression in the mattress, I found a seed like Jolene's, round and small as a sweet pea. I pinched it between my fingers and said, "Faith as small as a mustard seed can move mountains."

"Yes, that's what your sister always said."

"Is this one of Jolene's?"

My mother cupped the palm of her good hand, and I dropped the seed into it. She closed her fingers around it and said, "Yes. She liked to call it a mustard seed even though it isn't. I kept it all these years partly because it reminded me of her, and mostly because I kept telling myself if I believed just enough, had enough faith, that one day you'd come home."

I thought of the gravesite I had visited before coming to the house, the grass thick, the headstone faded, orange marigolds blooming nearby in a blue pot. Softly, in the early morning light, I had said, "Jolene, I have faith now. I hope you were right." To my mother, I asked, "Do you have another seed? I lost the one I had of Jolene's."

She stood up, reached for my hand, and took a step toward the bedroom door. "I think I just might. Why don't you come into the kitchen? Why don't we just see?"

Acknowledgments

Grateful acknowledgment is extended to the Albert P. Weisman Memorial Scholarship Fund at Columbia College Chicago for their generous support of this work.

I would like to offer many heartfelt thanks to: Randy Albers, Mort Castle, and Ann Hemenway, whose advice helped shape this book; Janet Britton, Jennifer Herder, Cindy Krause, Esther Krause, Hannah Krause, Sally Nalbor, and Theresa Raimonde, whose input was invaluable; Reba Osborne and Jotham Burrello, whose assistance helped me immensely in receiving funding for this project; and Werner Rauer, who spent his time and money helping me. Most of all, I'd like to thank my husband, Rollin, for believing in me, supporting me, and giving me the space I needed to write.

About the Author

Shelli Johnson is an award-winning journalist (sports reporting), novelist (grand prize winner), and blogger (shellijohnson.com/blog). She holds degrees in both journalism and fiction writing. She's also a truck owner, horse rider, dog lover, photographer, yoga enthusiast, and slow-cooker fan (shellijohnson.com/recipes). Find out more at: shellijohnson.com/about

Find out about Shelli's other books at:
shellijohnson.com/books

Visit: shellijohnson.com/signup
Opt-in for the newsletter to keep in touch.
Get your free stuff!

www.ingramcontent.com/pod-product-compliance
Lightning Source LLC
Chambersburg PA
CBHW021036130626
46552CB00005B/1873